Acclaim For T. C. Huo's first novel,

A Thousand Wings

"Huo writes with a surreal quality reminiscent of Jerzy Kosinski . . . His mouthwatering descriptions of egg rolls and pad thai are so vivid you want to find the nearest Asian restaurant. Throw in the history, politics, and culture of an exotic land, and you have a thoroughly rewarding novel."
—*USA Today*

"Simply splendid . . . a welcome new voice."
—*The Anniston Star*

"A Southeast Asian *Like Water for Chocolate*. Impressive . . . whets one's appetite for more of Huo's work."
—*Kirkus Reviews*

Born in Laos, **T. C. Huo** emigrated to the United States in 1979. He received his master's degree in creative writing from the University of California, Irvine. The author of *A Thousand Wings*, he lives in Santa Clara, California.

LAND OF SMILES

T. C. HUO

A PLUME BOOK

PLUME
Published by the Penguin Group
Penguin Putnam Inc., 375 Hudson Street,
New York, New York 10014, U.S.A.
Penguin Books Ltd, 27 Wrights Lane,
London W8 5TZ, England
Penguin Books Australia Ltd, Ringwood,
Victoria, Australia
Penguin Books Canada Ltd, 10 Alcorn Avenue,
Toronto, Ontario, Canada M4V 3B2
Penguin Books (N.Z.) Ltd, 182–190 Wairau Road,
Auckland 10, New Zealand

Penguin Books Ltd, Registered Offices:
Harmondsworth, Middlesex, England

First published by Plume,
a member of Penguin Putnam Inc.

First Printing, September, 2000
1 3 5 7 9 10 8 6 4 2

Copyright © T. C. Huo, 2000
All rights reserved

 REGISTERED TRADEMARK—MARCA REGISTRADA

LIBRARY OF CONGRESS CATALOGING-IN-PUBLICATION DATA:

Huo, T. C.
Land of smiles / T.C. Huo.
p.   cm.
ISBN 0-452-28185-7
1. Laotian Americans—Fiction.   2. Fathers and sons—Fiction.   3. Vietnamese Conflict,
1961–1975—Refugees—Fiction.   4. Emigration and immigration—Fiction.   5. Immigrants—
Fiction.   6. California—Fiction.   I. Title.
PS3558.U5314 L36 2000
813'.54—dc21   00-036720

Printed in the United States of America
Set in Palatino

PUBLISHER'S NOTE
This is a work of fiction. Names, characters, places, and incidents either are the products of
the author's imagination or are used fictitiously, and any resemblance to actual persons, living or dead, business establishments, events, or locales is entirely coincidental.

CONTENTS

LAND OF SMILES

PROLOGUE

The voice singing to his love on the other side of the border was familiar to many ears. The song: the radio played it, the jukebox played it. In the refugee camp as well as in downtown Nongkhai, patrons of the coffee shops fed coins to the jukebox to hear the singer sending his love across the Mekong to the woman he had left behind—a farm woman in a straw hat and sarong, a brown-faced woman who stood in the mist by the riverbank and looked across the Mekong to the border—to Nongkhai, Thailand. The Mekong, in Laos, flows from the north through my hometown, Luang Prabang, to the capital, and separates Laos from Thailand. In the late seventies, people got drowned, got shot as they tried to escape to Thailand. Some were caught and sent back; some were robbed and then murdered. The woman didn't know what had happened to her lover: whether he was saved, whether he had left the refugee camp and resettled in a third country, in America or Australia or France, whether he had married. She couldn't hear his song.

I bought the cassette in the refugee camp in Nongkhai, before I left for the States. Now listening to the song on the tape, I pictured this man. The cassette was old and poorly made. Almost all the songs had begun to blur: voices thickened, dragged out, twisted. But the male vigor in the song still sounded as tangible as the first time I heard it.

Hearing his voice now, listening to the tune, a young man, brown face and thick, inky-dark eyebrows, sprang from my head, flipped and somersaulted onto the Mekong riverbank, and stood astride, barefoot, by the water, his trousers—dark indigo, inky—rolled to his knees, his shirtsleeves—the same color as the trousers—rolled up to his elbows. He called her name.

A thick growth of shrubs with the roofs of two or three huts showing, coconut trees along the shore, occasionally the top of a Jeep making itself seen in the intervals between the shrubs as it drove by, a hawk suspending in the air: these were all he saw.

Someone remained deep behind those shrubs. A mere speck. Deaf to the call, deaf to her name.

He didn't know what had happened to her. That night he turned his back on her, walked out of the door. If he'd made it across the border, why couldn't he have taken her along? The song omitted why the man left his woman behind.

There were bachelors in the camp, many of them young men by themselves without family and without money. They swam across the river, and if they had girlfriends, their girlfriends either couldn't swim at all or couldn't swim the whole stretch. So these men swam across the river to be bachelors.

Many women let their men go while they stayed and waited, either because they could not swim, or even if they could, it was inconceivable that they be on their own in the refugee camp—how could they manage? Either they married a *farang* or a Thai, probably a colonel or a lieutenant, someone with a star badge on his shoulder and a gun tucked in his belt, someone who could get them out of the camp and make them a legitimate Thai housewife. Otherwise they would be stuck in the camp for years and years and there would be no way of ever getting out. A young woman drowned herself in a pond in the camp because her aunt, on the list to go to France, could not take her along.

Because of this, many women had to stay in Laos. Not my mother though. She didn't wait. To this day I still did not know what made her, or why she would, take such an action on her own. She crossed the river with my seven-year-old sister. They left my father in Luang Prabang without his knowledge. They left home for the Land of Smiles.

Your mama missed you, Ahma told me. For several months she didn't know what happened to you in Thailand. We had no news, no letter. She missed you so badly she had to go to Thailand to look for you.

What puzzled me was that my mother would take such a grave matter upon herself without consulting my father, the head of the household, and leave the country by herself, keeping her thoughts from him. Had he known them, he would have seen to the matter, he would have prearranged a passage. Perhaps he knew her thoughts all along but did nothing about them.

I didn't remember having ever seen my parents sit down and discuss matters with each other. My father was always busy, first with the woodshop and then with the volunteer work. After the Communist takeover, he spent almost all his time on community work, always more involved in the community activities than in our family, oblivious to our future.

He dismissed my mother's thoughts. He told her again and again to wait for the right moment—for a few more months. A few months turned into another year. Fed up, she packed and left.

That they had an argument and that she, in anger, took my sister and flew to Vientiane, the capital, seemed unlikely. I didn't remember having seen my parents argue. She had never argued with him although she might have been unhappy about him. Plus, he always kept the welfare of the family in mind. He cared for my Ahma, my mother, my sister, and me. He really had the best intentions, I had to believe that. When my mother gave birth to my sister in the hospital he took care of her day and night. He found her the best doctor. He slept by her bedside. He gave her a blood transfusion. That she would cross the border to Thailand without his knowledge was impossible.

If he knew, would he let her cross the river by herself? How would she keep it from him? Impossible. She must have told him. The rationale: a house with its doors shut, its windows closed and blinds pulled down, would cause suspicion. It was safer to let my mother and my sister leave first, my father and Ahma would follow later. But at the time he and Grandma were still at our home in Luang Prabang, whereas my mother was in Vientiane, where she contacted the boatman.

My father got the news in Luang Prabang. It's the Moon Festival, a family friend, Mrs. Lee, told me in the camp. Your father was at the community association with us when the telegram came. He burst into tears.

If he knew my mother planned to leave the country, the day she crossed the Mekong he would be in Vientiane with her and my sister. He would have made arrangements for them. He would have seen them off. He would have seen the boatman and known where he could be found. Not to have done so was out of character.

So, he didn't know. Through her friends who also planned on leaving, my mother found the contact and took out her purse. My friends and their families all crossed the border together and entered the refugee camp together. Other families, four or five members more than mine, big families, had reached Thailand safely. It did not make sense that it was hard for my family of four members, not counting me, to flee the country together. I found it hard to accept.

In the camp, I chanced upon my father's letter to my maternal uncle in California. My father wrote, *Thy sister had followed the big river eastward,* and other expressions of grief which I found formal, stylized, and awkward. My father never found my mother's body. The gold and the jewelry weighed her down, Ahma said. My mother sank down to the river floor. I saw her flowing southbound, passing villages, passing under the villagers' eyes, passing from one province to the next, kilometers away from home.

By the time my father and the rescue team arrived, a day or two later, they were too late: she had flowed into Cambodia. A fisherman had caught sight of her, a lump of something bobbing along in the turbidity of the current. Facedown, her back turned to the sky. But standing akimbo in his sarong he watched her float by, didn't bother to do anything other than watch. In the rainy season when the river welled up, he had seen trees, dogs, pigs, and water buffalo rolling along the current, bloated beings.

My mother had even passed the singer by the bank at the Thai side of the river. As he sang about how much he missed his loved one still remaining in Laos, ten feet from him, the current turned and pushed my mother. In the middle of the song, he saw a tree trunk—or a bundle of clothing—uncertain as to which way to drift. Perhaps a fisherman, having found her floating along, was kind enough to salvage her body, and buried her.

Had my father spread the word? Village after village if necessary. From one province to the next. All the way from the capital to the southern tip of Laos so that everyone along the river would be on the lookout for my mother? No. I asked for too much. My father did all he could. He covered the area where the boat capsized. He found my sister's body.

Ahma and family friends—like Mrs. Lee—believed that my mother had sunk. The bracelets and necklaces and those gold chains she carried were too heavy. My sister did not sink, and my father found her.

I couldn't see my mother, a person of simplicity, wearing all that jewelry, as Mrs. Lee claimed. True, my mother had many pieces—and they were heavy. Perhaps she put them in small pouches and fastened them with safety pins to her pockets. She took her life's fortune with her, Mrs. Lee whispered to other housewives.

As for the boatman, he fled, Ahma told me. I couldn't imagine why he would flee without taking the jewelry from the passengers, all women and children. After all, he sank them. He tipped over the boat. Perhaps he had even bashed the passengers with the oar, the children and the women screaming and crying, panicking, tilting the boat from left to right, right to left. He threatened them. With a knife. With a gun. He bashed the young woman whom the young man sang about. He bashed my mother.

It happened near the shore, Ahma said. The boat had barely started off but the water was already deep—above the head. The boat had barely started off before the boatman tipped it. He robbed them and then sank the boat, near the shore.

Nobody saw what happened? Nobody heard any screams? I glanced at my grandmother.

It happened at two in the afternoon. There was not a soul around, she said.

Two o'clock. Not a leaf, not a grass blade stirred on the bank. The coconut trees along the shore stood still. Mutely, the Mekong kept moving south. A leaflike object, slender and long, disappearing into the brown torrent. Ants in the swirl, arms thrashing, heads half lifting. Some faint cry? An uneven surface, wild rippling.

Remember the family who sold café at the corner of the market? I shook my head and said I forgot. The two boys in that family made it to the shore, Ahma said. They were with their mother. With the exception of those two brothers, the boatful of women and children—none of them survived.

No man with them?

None. All women and children. That's why the boatman robbed them. He knew none of them could swim, Ahma said.

I remembered, vaguely, what the older brother looked like, but I doubted if the figure I conjured up was the right one. I remembered seeing him in school in Luang Prabang, an eight-year-old with a crew cut, two or three grades lower than mine. I had never talked to him. I had not even seen him in the camp, although Ahma told me that he was in the camp too, with his younger brother. I had never seen them—but if I did, what would I say to them? We would say nothing to each other. I wondered if they told my father what they had seen.

It now occurred to me that the boatman could have been a Lao instead of a Thai. All along I thought a Thai had committed this crime. He got away. No Lao or Thai police tracking him down. No attempt to arrest him because how was it possible? Not Thai citizens, we had no recourse to hunt him down in Thailand, no recourse to justice.

But even if the boatman was Lao, I suspected my father and other bereft husbands had to keep silent. How could they tell the Pathet Lao that their wives and children had tried to escape the Communist regime and cross the border and as a result were drowned. My father would get in trouble. I suspected that he conducted the search clandestinely, not daring to breathe a word to the police or the soldiers, asking them to help search for the bodies and arrest the boatman—bring him to death.

The search: small-scale. It was all my father could muster. Having found my sister, he and the other widowers, or some villagers, kept on with the search. It couldn't go on too long if my mother would not surface.

She must have been somewhere else. I'd thought that since my father had not found her, she must have been saved. A fisherman in a small village in Laos had rescued her, and all along she had tried to find a way to cross the Mekong again, to get some news of us and to get some news across—that she was alive, that we should take her along and get her out. She was somewhere along the river, her gold and addresses lost. And yet we left her behind.

NEW ARRIVAL

⁓

The day had been blustery. The leaves of the lone papaya tree near the front of the refugee camp folded and bent in the direction of the hissing wind. Trash like the plastic bags, cigarette butts, and drinking straws had blown off somewhere, so that the entrance to the refugee camp looked bald and deserted, just a broad stretch of bare reddish-brown earth, and pebbles. It looked like there was nothing between the sky and the earth, except the papaya tree, and the sign that read LAO REFUGEE CAMP, and the haze that hovered over the landscape, made fuzzy by the passage of twenty some years. Given another twenty years, the image of the camp would have shrunk to just the sign.

Now, in California, in 1999, I could still say with a degree of certainty that the sign painted in Thai and English, and the nearby lone papaya tree, with leaves swaying in the gust which had cleaned up the camp by blowing away any trash to reveal the reddish composition of the surface of the earth, were exactly what the stranger had seen on that blustery day, with no haze to obscure his vision. The stranger must have known his way, because he stepped around the painted sign to enter the camp, and found his way through the myriad alleys, rows of huts, curious children gawking at him, one or two arrogant rooters crossing his path, to show up at my door with a letter from my father.

I had been in the camp in Ubon, an eastern province of Thailand, for seven months. I stayed in a shack with a few people. In the first four months I wrote to my mother often. My letters betrayed my anxiety about my situation, about staying in the refugee camp by myself. My mother wrote back, enclosed some money, told me to contact my dear uncle in California. Yes, my mother's brother and my father's sister, all in America, I could count on as a backup.

Then the letters stopped. For three months I did not hear from my mother. I continued to write, but received no response.

Until the messenger showed up. With the letter.

It had always been my mother who wrote, so I found it odd that the letter came from my father. He informed me of my family's safe arrival in the refugee camp in Nongkhai province. The messenger would take me to join them there. This piece of news brought an end to my anxiety and uncertainty.

The messenger, a dark-complected man—a former soldier, I later learned—told me he would handle the matter about my departure with the camp official. We would leave the next morning.

I had only a few items of clothing, a sweater that a granny was kind enough to give me as the weather turned chilly. Anxious to get going, I went to bed early that night.

I didn't know what the messenger had said to the camp officials, how he explained my departure, but true to his words, the officials let me go without trouble. As far as they were concerned, I had never stayed in the camp in Ubon. I was free to start anew as a fugitive. They didn't keep a tight record of who came in and who got out. I had known a few people who registered in the camp as refugees and then moved out to stay in the center of town, where they acted as and passed for the Thai, and would return to the camp only for periodic roll calls.

We left for the bus depot mid-morning. The bus took us through different provinces, steadily heading north. I wished the bus would have the speed of an aircraft.

When we arrived in the Nongkhai bus depot, it was getting dark, almost five. I put on my sweater. We took a taxi and before long it dropped us off in a narrow street with shops. The messenger walked me to a truck parked on the street. A man signaled for passengers to finish their last-minute business and get on, waving his hand as he stood outside the truck, in twilight. We squeezed into the crowded truck. The man collected the fares and slammed the door, got on the driver's seat and started the engine.

Because of the cold wind sweeping in, the passengers huddled quietly. The truck was the only vehicle running on the long straightaway across the dark open space. Looking out the truck, I saw the stars beginning to appear. They hung far above the open field, above rice paddies in the mist. In Southeast Asia, mid-November seems the deep of winter, the air hushed with chill, the land a great span of dormancy, silent. Unknown kilometers spun out dark and misty ahead of me. The cold wind brushed my face and hair and the sky was a deep lake-bottom blue. The stars became brighter and bigger. Then I saw, far below them and out in the field, spots of light. A moment later, a row of houses, or shacks, or huts, came into view. I asked the escort at my side, Is that the refugee camp? Are we getting there now?

The truck slowed down, made a right turn, and came to a stop. The wind died down accordingly. The passengers began to get off and head to the lighted entrance. The messenger took the bundle of my clothing and we headed to the entrance, which turned out to be a checkpoint. The messenger presented a pass to the guards at the checkpoint and spoke a few words to them. Without any questions the guards let us in.

We crossed the checkpoint and entered the camp. I took a deep breath. At last, in a matter of minutes, I would reunite with my family. I looked about me. The messenger waved to a cabman who pedaled forward, toward us. The messenger put the bundle of my clothing in the center of the pedal cab and we got on and sat by the side on the passenger seat. It was the first time I saw this type of pedal cab, which had five wheels and no protective covering, so that if it rained, the passengers would sure get drenched. It was not the kind of three-wheel paddle cab found in Laos.

The cabman started to pedal and the wind rose after us. I pulled my shirt collar together. The pedal cab bumped along the unpaved road, passing rows of lighted barracks. An orange world, the incandescent glow of warmth. After passing a row of barracks and shacks, the cab stopped.

The messenger pointed it out to me: the hut, where I would find my family. I hurried in.

The hut was empty and dark. I did not see my mother or Ahma making dinner in the kitchen—where was the kitchen? No coals glowing in the stove. No spatula scraping the wok as Ahma stirred the vegetables and pork sizzling in there. I smelled no rice or food that indicated my family were waiting for me to start dinner. Strange. Just when I thought I was in the wrong household, Ahma emerged from darkness. She shuffled forward and gripped my hands. Her hands felt chapped.

Ahma! I cried out. So I was in the right place. Mother? Where is Mother? And Sister? I looked about me again and again, thinking that they must be somewhere in the back, as Ahma held on to my hands. Where are they?

Ahma lighted a candle on a table, then bade me to sit down. The escort took leave. I sat by the door of what turned out to be the bedroom. Ahma sat down on a low stool. She said she had things to tell me. She bade me not to cry, yet tears streamed in her eyes and down her cheeks as she talked about the Mekong. I became quiet. She kept wiping her eyes with a handkerchief. I leaned against the bamboo pole and stared at the candle. Ahma's voice seemed to come from somewhere far away. I heard words: stony, metallic.

I began to cry after Ahma was already asleep next to me. I tried to stifle my sobbing, for fear of waking her up, and when I turned around to wipe my eyes, I saw my father, sound and whole, sleeping next to Ahma under the same blanket. For the whole evening he had disappeared somewhere and came back only after Ahma and I were already asleep. Looking away from him, I stared at the row of thatches, whose straws swayed in the direction of the wind. My sight became blurry. Tears wet my pillow.

Sometime later, in my fitful sleep, a loud noise startled me, tin buckets knocking against each other loudly, or against some hard surface like cement. Then Ahma explained, It's only the sound of people getting water. She pulled the blanket up my chin and told me to sleep on. As I closed my eyes, tears again rolled onto my pillow. It must have been four o'clock. Still too dark to see anything.

After a while, the noise, the buckets knocking against each other and against the well, died down. When I woke up again, I heard a song, someone listening to the radio. Probably a neighbor who got up to boil drinking water for the day. It was a man singing a slow Thai song. I began to cry again, soundlessly, breathing through my mouth. A breeze swept into the hut, lifting some of the straws on the thatches. Only then did I know what it was like to delve into my liver and heart, dig them out, to delve into the bottomless sorrow that would stay with me forever.

I surveyed my surroundings that morning. It was not exactly a hut, but an annex, with three families in it, including mine. Ahma said my father had helped build it. He was a home-builder by trade. The straw thatches still retained the color of the hay, fresh and tawny, not yet dust-laden or sun-baked. The bedroom stood one foot above the ground, on stilts. The wickerwork floor, made of pliant bamboo sticks, formed what looked like a mat. The same wickerwork made up the walls, or partitions. Another family lived one partition away. Ahma had glued sheets of newspapers to the walls to cover the slits formed by the wickerwork. A layer or two of straw thatches made up the roof. Four bamboo poles supported the bedroom. More of my father's handiwork: the newly cemented floor in the living-room area, untrampled, bark green, so clean I hardly dared walk on it. The kitchen, two feet wide, five feet long, was mounted over a gutter alongside the living-room area. The bath stall was on the other end of the kitchen, next to the neighbor's bedroom. Behind which were two rows of outhouses for the entire barrack. The annex was an extension of barrack number twelve. Each barrack housed about forty families. I refused to think of the annex as "home."

In Laos, when I was very young, I used to point out our house with a mango tree on one side, and a guava tree on the other, to my mother's good friend Mrs. Lee. When she came to see my mother for a hairdo, she liked to ask me simple questions just to hear me talk. I'd told her, This is my home and this is my family. I mentioned Ahma, my parents, my baby sister. I didn't know that one day I would have nothing to point to, or worth pointing to.

So, I saw the annex—this extension to Barrack 12—merely as a place to stay, to sleep in, nothing more. I was merely a sojourner.

Standing on the cold cement floor, Ahma, huddled in her deep brown corduroy jacket, pointed to the corrugated tin wall. The well is right next to this wall on the outside, she said.

I wanted to know who shared the annex with us.

She teaches French. A masterly French speaker. She used to teach in a *collège*. We call her Madame Françoise, Ahma said.

Madame Françoise? Is she French?

No. We gave her that name because she has a Ph.D. You can learn French from her, Ahma added.

I met Madame Françoise later in the day. Her voice heralded her arrival even before I saw her person. A woman's voice asked, Is this your grandson? And with the voice came the person. She padded toward Ahma and spoke before Ahma had a chance to. Poor child. Sit down here. Let Madame take a good look at you.

I took a good look at her too: she had a stumpy figure; her short hands outside the sleeves of her egg-yolk-yellow blouse and short legs below the folds of a frayed sarong recalled sections of a thick sausage. She had a puffy hairdo, and as she came near I smelled a heavy dose of hair spray. I recognized her. I had seen her a few times in my old hometown.

She held my hands as we each sat on a low stool. She let out a series of soft exclamations, what I took to be French. Then she uttered in Lao, My poor child. She pulled me close, and if I had not pulled back, for she was not my mother or grandmother, I would have tumbled onto her bosom.

From now on we'll take good care of you. Her voice was warm, and full of genuine concern. My eyes began to water. I live in the same hut, she said, pointing to her door. We're the same family now. Ask Madame if you ever need anything. Promise? She patted my back. To start out, Madame will take you to a French breakfast tomorrow. Still remember the French pastry we had in Laos? You can have that too.

I glanced at Ahma, not knowing what to say. I liked Madame Françoise already.

Around five or six o'clock in the morning, a bullhorn used as a loudspeaker broadcast my name. Boontakorn. It traveled far and clear, spreading from the administration building to the rest of the camp. It roused me from my sleep. I woke up, confused and perplexed.

The announcement urged the people on the list to go to France to meet at the front of the administration building. The broadcaster continued to read out names on the departure list. The Darasuk family. The Minaykone. Mr. Boonsing. But my father did not apply to go to France. Someone else must have the same name as mine. I slept on.

Soon after the broadcast, I began to hear jogging, right outside, toward the hut. I kept my eyes closed. It was a comforting sound because it sounded just like the orderly jogging of soldiers past our house at the crack of dawn, every morning, back in Laos. The orderly crunching of boots, the whistling of the captain, just before the sky turned fish-belly white. Now, in the refugee camp in Thailand, there was a lone jogger still keeping up with the regimen of morning exercise, likewise before the sky turned fish-belly white. The sound of jogging became distant and soon passed out of hearing.

Café Français was situated in a far corner of the camp, facing a dusty open space. The French restaurant completely lacked the grandeur I had expected. Café Français was a hut with a thatched roof made of straw, the bare earth served as the floor. Other facts: Café Français was the only French restaurant in the camp. Café Français did not serve coffee or pastry. The tableware of Café Français included a set of knife, spoon, and fork.

Madame nonetheless pressed me to order as much food as I wanted. I asked for a cup of Ovaltine. No, Café Français did not serve Ovaltine. I asked for bread with pâté. The waitress returned to the interior of the restaurant to relay my request. A dark scrawny man, whom I took to be the grand chef, parted the curtain in the doorway and poked his head through. There were only two customers. He returned to the seclusion of the kitchen. I glanced at Madame. Did Café Français serve any food?

The waitress parted the curtain holding in her hand a tin

plate with two yellow, sickly-looking baguettes. When she presented the bread, she said she had no pâté. So I asked for *jell-bong*, ground chili spread, with thin strips of pork skin, which I had in Laos. Freshly baked bread, with slices of Vietnamese pork loaf, with a thin smear of *jell-bong* to lend pungency. Yes, Café Français most definitely had *jell-bong* spread, but without the other integral ingredient: the thin strips of chewy, tough pork skin.

I didn't care for the food—but not because it wasn't French. I simply lacked the appetite. We returned to the hut.

As we passed the morning market, Madame urged me to talk as much as befit her, she being single, idea of a child, an earthly monkey with brio, but I lacked the inclination. I was bound in the muteness of the universe, eternal, unearthly, and everywhere.

Mid-morning. My father covered the floor with a few sheets of newspapers. He stood on them, in front of a book-size mirror hung on the wall, by the door. He opened a small package with some Japanese words on it, from which he took out a tube that resembled toothpaste. He uncapped it, and squeezed the contents on a comb, and proceeded to comb his hair. Tiny drops of black dye stained the newspapers under his feet. He combed the substance into his hair until it turned sleek, and blacker than mine.

Never, never did it occur to me that his hair needed dying, for I took it as a given that a father should have some gray hair.

I sat waiting in the doorway of the bedroom, my feet dangling off the stilted floor. Then I heard Ahma, who was in the bedroom, call my mother's name, Are you coming to see your son? Look after him, she said to my mother. And then Ahma called my sister, You must miss him, coming to see your brother.

I was startled. Two praying mantes crawled slowly up the bamboo pole, the smaller one following her mother. To see them, I had to follow where Ahma was looking when she spoke.

She talked to the praying mantes, Coming back to see us? You want to be with us? You want to— She took out her damp handkerchief.

The two praying mantes crawled ahead, going away slowly, each carrying a heavy bundle of grief on her back.

Shh, don't stir, you will chase it away, Ahma said in a soft voice as she kept her eyes on the insects. Then I saw the meaning of it. I remained still. As I watched the praying mantes while Ahma kept mumbling, I was quickly losing self-control. The praying mantes took a step up and all at once my sight blurred.

I rushed to the bathing stall and splashed a scoop of water from the tank on my face to cool my eyes. I wiped my face on a towel, took a deep breath, and when I was sufficiently calm, returned to the bedroom.

As I stood still, careful not to accidentally step on the visitors, I found none. My eyes roamed over the mosquito net, around the suitcases, up the bamboo post, along the wall. In the doorway, I lay down on my stomach and looked under the stilted floor. The praying mantes were gone.

My father had finished dyeing his hair and was now cleaning the area. He dropped the package and the empty tube on the pile of stained newspapers and squatted to roll the newspapers up.

Ahma was cooking in the kitchen.

As I leaned on the doorway, I conjured up the image of the praying mantes climbing up the leg of my pants. I watched the insects, feigning unawareness, while making an effort to get in touch with them.

My father proceeded to blow-dry his hair.

Someone stepped in.

Ahma looked out from behind the bamboo partition.

The man, who could be Thai and as such enjoyed the privilege of legitimate citizenship, or a Lao who had adopted Thai citizenship, asked if we wanted to buy a TV set. Not knowing how to say no to a salesperson, my father, his hair still wet, asked the man about the cost, as if interested in buying.

Ahma said a TV set sounded ideal, except there was no place to put it.

Would you want to try it for ten days?

There's another problem, my father said. Lately the electricity has been cut off in the early evenings. I am afraid it'll have to wait until next time.

When you need a TV, anytime you need one, I am available, the salesman said with a half-hopeful, half-pleading smile and a tone of voice to match. He stepped out of the hut.

I peered at the legs of my pants to see if there were any praying mantes.

Ahma set the table for lunch. She didn't make a lot. Two panfried mackerels, steamed water spinach, a saucer of sauce, a bowl of wintermelon soup. We sat, three generations around the table. Not a forlorn sight to outsiders. We ate without talking. I didn't see any praying mantes or grasshoppers. Not even an ant.

After lunch my father took me downtown. We purchased two passes—costing a baht each—from the Thai guard at the gate of the camp, and waited outside for a passenger truck.

The truck arrived, shooting up a screen of dust. Without regard for hygiene, the dust spread wide and closed in on us and imposed its unwanted presence on our faces and clothes. The people waiting by the roadside covered their noses and mouths. Even as passengers got off, we swarmed toward the truck.

The straightaway cut through the plain—the dry rice field, the desolate countryside—between the camp and downtown Nongkhai. As I looked out the truck, I touched my sweater. It felt solid, but provided comfort of only a meager sort. The sight of the open countryside devoid of human presence resonated more with my spirits.

The two-story shops and houses, some with large awnings, on both sides of the narrow street in downtown, looked like the place where the escort and I, on the evening we arrived, got off the taxi and hastened to board the passenger truck about to depart.

He took me to a bank—which looked like an old villa, with the serenity of a temple—near the end of the street. He took out the safe that he'd rented, and showed me its contents. I recognized my sister's gold bracelets and some of my mother's rings in the metal box. The foreign, dark cold metal box. Since my arrival in the camp, he had not mentioned a word. He now showed me where my sister's bracelets and my mother's rings ended up. The long cold metal box shaped like a coffin: that should be explanation enough. I nodded. He knew how to get a safe in a bank without knowing how to speak and read Thai. It was comforting to know that he was a resourceful, competent man.

We took a side street and sauntered to the Mekong—so near downtown, it turned out.

The water level had risen, the whole river welling up. When I swam across the border, in late April, the river was quite shallow and calm, so shallow that small sand dunes surfaced, so calm that it replaced my fear with hope. The monsoon would yet arrive. The coolness of the water teased into my legs and the mud tickled my soles. I felt thrilled, for I was running away from home with my schoolfellows. I was about to put Laos behind me, me between the Mekong and the unknown ahead of me. Knee-deep, I kept going deeper. As the water reached my waist, I lifted my hands up. The sun shone into my eyes and the waves ahead of me broke into sparkling gold bars that bobbed and shifted. The water reached my chest. I put my hands one over the other, like the mouth of an arrow, and dove headlong in the direction of the Land of Smiles, my feet making white splashes. Before long my hands stirred up sand that clouded around me as I plowed ahead. I stood up and my feet touched soft mud. I found myself already past the middle of the river, closer to the Thai side of the border than to Laos. I turned to look at my classmates alongside me. We exchanged glances. Once this far, it would be too late to turn back, too dangerous. I might get caught or shot. My heart began to pound wildly. I kept swimming.

Before the emancipation in 1975, when we were in Vientiane, my parents took me to eateries on the riverfront. On the open-air patios, we watched the view as we drank sweetened red iced tea, sampled raw papaya salad and skewers of coal-roasted dried beef jerky with sticky rice. Boats slowly (as if the clock had stopped ticking) and freely (as if no border existed) traversed the water, back and forth between Laos and Thailand. People from Vientiane even took trips to spend a day in Nongkhai and returned to Vientiane on the same day. The evening breeze off the river created a welcome sensation, and I, on my mother's lap, gazed across the gleaming water toward the opposite shore, toward Nongkhai, Thailand.

Now in Nongkhai, my father and I looked across the broad span of brown frothing swelling wrathful currents, toward Vientiane, Laos. The opposite shore appeared like a reflection of this side of the shore where my father and I stood gazing: spots of wooden houses on stilts behind the coconut trees and bushes and bamboo forest. The same vegetation. The same climate. The same customs. Herein lay the difference: neither humans nor boats were in sight.

MATCHMAKING

In January, Madame Françoise converted the living room we were supposed to share into a classroom. Upon her neighborly request, my father put his carpenter skills to use: he made a chalkboard, nailed it outside her bedroom, and installed three rows of benches which took up half the living-room space. A table behind the benches became the place for meals.

For his work, she thanked him, calling him her Big Brother, a compliment that never failed to flatter a man, pumping up his sense of masculinity.

After rallying enough students, from ages ten to fifty, Madame Françoise launched her enterprise. She would teach the youngsters in the daytime. I look forward to their lively chanting of the alphabet, she told Ahma. The youngsters' mothers composed the other half of the student population, who would come for their lessons at night, to learn French for their future resettlement in France or Canada.

At seven o'clock on the first night of class, fifteen housewives filed into the hut. I knew most of them—I called them aunties—because we came from the same town. Among them were the wives of the managers and representatives of the overseas Chinese association. Some of them, such as Mrs. Lee, my mother's good friend, used to play with me whenever they visited my mother's hair parlor.

In Laos, Mrs. Lee came to our home regularly to have her hair styled. My mother took out a tray of scissors, clips, razors, hair rollers, and bottles of strong-smelling liquid. My three-year-old sister sang outside the parlor as my mother shampooed Mrs. Lee. My sister sang and played piano—the small table where Ahma put the rice cooker became the makeshift piano, the edge of the table the keys. My sister alternated her fingers from thumb to index, her hands and her body swaying with the song. She had wrapped a towel around her waist, over her pants, and the towel became her costume, a gold-pleated sarong. The entire house became her stage. After a song, my sister stopped and slipped off the stool and trotted into the parlor. What a sweet voice. Such lovely singing. Who taught you? Mrs. Lee asked my sister as my mother squeezed a bottle of liquid on the curlers in her hair. Tell your dad to buy an organ for you, Mrs. Lee suggested. She's too young for an organ. We'll wait until she's older, my mother said. What's this? Mrs. Lee pointed at the towel around my sister's waist. My sister grinned, her dimples showing. It's my Lao skirt, she said. A Lao skirt? You look like a Japanese doll, Mrs. Lee remarked. My sister chuckled. She sat down on a stool. Where are your Japanese clothes? Don't have any, my sister said. She looks so much like a Japanese doll, Mrs. Lee told my mother. People say she looks Japanese. Hey, Japanese doll, Mrs. Lee teased my sister. Mrs. Lee was no stranger to my family.

Now, in the refugee camp, she came to Madame Françoise for French lessons. Some aunties spoke both Lao and Mandarin, mixing the two in their phrases and questions. Some of them learned French and English at the same time. They attributed their difficulty in learning a new language to the regression of their memory. As Madame walked to become the center of the class, stopping in front of the chalkboard, Mrs. Lee, seated among the students in the front row, complained, We keep forgetting the raw words, Madame.

It'll take some time for the grammar to take root, Madame Françoise said. Weary, Madame let this bland speech substitute for her usual brittle wit. She did not expect her students, almost half a century old, to study as hard as she expected their children to. In the daytime her adult students earned their living in the market as vendors of mosquito coils, toilet paper, batteries, flashlights, tiger balms. Under the weak giddy incandescent light, Madame began the first lesson: the first seven letters of the alphabet.

Every day, even before I finished lunch, the kids began to show up. They rushed in and out every hour or so, from morning till late afternoon. No use telling them to wait outside until their official lesson time. They darted in and, halfway in the door, threw their books like flying saucers across the room onto the bench to claim a seat, and dashed out, shrieking with the lawlessness of barbarians. A few students stayed inside, eyeing me munching sticky rice and a piece of fried pork lung.

I was aware of the kids staring at me with the hungry eyes of tigers, ready at any moment to jump for my seat. I rushed to finish my lunch, to chew quickly and gulp, not caring what I ate as long as it filled my stomach. Swallowing the last mouthful, I put the bowl and the plate of fried pork lung in the kitchen. And as I turned around to clean the table, the little tigers had already crowded there, the crown spot of the classroom, because it was at the very back, and the farthest from the teacher.

More tigers arrived. More noises, higher volume.

After cleaning the table, I went into the bedroom. I began to sweat, but found it impossible to take a nap. I tried to study, but was distracted by the hums and chants—bee drones from forty kids packed in that space. Even as they droned, the kids of the next session began poking their heads through the door, and quickly becoming bolder, they stepped in, and soon began to chatter among themselves, leaning on the bamboo partition and the door.

Behind the bedroom door, I sweated frantically, first cursing my karma for the impossibility of either sleeping or studying my English vocabulary at that moment, then cursing the sun for shining so pitilessly above me and all over the camp, cursing the way I heard Ahma and my mother and my aunts and others curse their fate over and over.

I unlatched the door and pushed it against the wall of talking-away kids not much shorter than I, not caring if I pushed them over, not caring if they fell. But to my surprise, the door remained immovable. I peeked through the bamboo slits of the door: a couple of kids pressed on it still, blabbing away. I pushed harder and stepped out, without giving the kids I had pushed aside so much as a glance. The room had become a jungle. I fought my way through.

All I wanted was a place to simply station my body. Lacking this, the next best thing was to keep moving. I took the backstreet that surrounded the entire camp in a rectangle: first I passed the vocational school near the hut, went all the way until the road ended, then I turned right, headed toward and passed the administration building at the front of the camp, and when the road ended I turned right, headed toward and passed the old cemetery, a marsh where the coffins soaked in stagnant water, the graves all muddy. With half of the graves removed, the excavation continued even in the daytime. It was necessary to move the coffins to a dry place. I passed the church and the slaughterhouse, and turned right toward the market.

In the beginning I made one round. But the class did not end until two hours later. I made another round. And another. I wished the camp had more alleys, more hospitals, more markets, more shops, so I could walk endlessly, because Madame Françoise had turned the living-room area into a school, seven hours a day, two hours in the morning, three hours in the afternoon, two hours at night.

Other people too walked from barrack to barrack, to coffee-houses, to the market. There were always people milling in the alleys, in different corners of the camp, day and night, day after day. I never lacked company. With so many people circling the camp with me, I remained conveniently hidden from family friends who would otherwise see me pass by their units.

I became driven by the need to walk. Every day, right after lunch, I went on the walking tour. One day I found a resting area, a small pavilion where the five-wheeled-pedicab drivers stopped by for a cigarette. I stayed there till four, until I was sure all the ant and tiger scholars had disbanded.

From that day on, the pavilion became the place where I came to rest my feet. Usually I was the only one there. On one occasion a wrinkled, thin hunchback came in and sat by the steps smoking a pipe. And once, a Hmong woman came in to breast-feed a baby.

In the evening, Mrs. Lee came to class with a few other housewives. While the women chatted with Ahma in the bedroom before the class started, Mrs. Lee pulled me to a corner and asked me where my father was.

I don't—

An auntie at the bench cut me off. Why isn't he in? She exchanged a look with Mrs. Lee—eyes that passed secrets to each other. Were the two complicit in a scheme and hiding it from me?

We haven't seen him lately, Mrs. Lee said. Maybe he's seeing a woman? As they tried to wheedle information from me, they got bolder in their insinuations. They blatantly passed eye messages to each other.

I wished they would leave me alone. But since they were

my elders, I could only listen obediently and not talk back. If I told them to go away or else shut up, I would give them more to blab about: they would say I was impolite, undisciplined, brazen—a brat. So I suffered the smell of Mrs. Lee's hair spray.

After the class started, with the mothers droning the French alphabet after Madame Françoise a door away, it became impossible for me to study in the hut under the candlelight. I considered enrolling in a night class myself. It would give me a place to go to after dinner, a place to station my body.

It felt comfortable to walk in the dark alleys. No one could recognize me. I walked up the alley between Barracks 12 and 13, reached the main street. The coffee stalls and eateries and convenience stores at the front of the alleys along the main street were lit up. People milled about on the street. I crossed it, jumped over the ditch to the sandy athletic field. After I crossed it to get to the other side of the camp, I jumped over the ditch onto the main street (it enclosed the athletic field in a rectangle). I stayed away from the cemetery and went to the pond instead, across from the cemetery, at the edge of the athletic field. Dots of illumination flew over the pond. Firebugs.

I walked in dark or dimly lit alleys—each alley was between two barracks—from barracks one to forty, one round after another until the last French class was over at nine.

One day, after dinner, Ahma went to see a friend of hers. Soon after she left, Mrs. Lee and other housewives with exercise books in their hands arrived. I stayed in the bedroom, with the door closed.

Where did you get such a beautiful hairdo? I heard Madame Françoise ask.

It's not too puffy? Mrs. Lee's answer-as-question somehow made it clear that she was immoderately flattered.

Through the tiny space between the door and the pole, I could see her patting her hairdo, turning this way and that.

It fits you perfectly, added Madame in a nakedly goading tone.

I still think my hairdresser overdid it this time. Mrs. Lee let out a soft sigh.

It's beautiful. More insincere praise.

Nowadays, in this camp, where can we go to get a nice hairdo? a housewife said, in a way that made it unclear whether she was asking Mrs. Lee for a recommendation or was lamenting the lack of beauty shops, in fact making a social observation.

You're right. Is there a decent place? Madame Françoise said. It makes it hard to take care of one's hair. And what for? In this refugee camp, I simply ignore my hair. It can grow which way it wants.

You are wrong there, Madame. If any of us should take care of our hair, you would be the one, said Mrs. Lee. For us married housewives, family comes first, but it's a different matter for you.

Indeed, hair is one of a single woman's most important assets, another housewife said.

Madame is the Ph.D among us. Her mind is her asset.

That's why a hairdo can be an asset piled on another asset. A rose in full bloom needs a vase.

Amid general laughter, Madame blushed, and could only say lamely, I can't afford a perm, unconvinced of her own words even as she said them.

Madame is going to France to marry a *farang,* someone said.

Only a European can truly appreciate Madame's mind, said another.

And her hair!

They burst into loud guffaw.

Still laughing, Mrs. Lee said, Madame is the wise one among us. She understands the value of hair, which is ephemeral. Black one year, gray the next.

You are denying yourself, Madame. Look at Mrs. Lee. With a new hairdo, doesn't she look like she's still twenty-something?

Surely you jest, Mrs. Lee protested happily, determined to negate all compliments about her hair.

I can't stop admiring your hair, Mrs. Lee, Madame exclaimed, bending over to touch it with a suddenness and force that seemed to indicate she wished to mess it up into a dirty bird's nest.

From their chitchat I learned that they took it upon themselves, knowing that a single man was always in need of a wife, to fix my father up with a woman and then unite the two dry bundles of kindling with fire.

They ruled out young unmarried women and widows with the burden of children, and focused on those in middle age, single, with looks that would help advance the future husband's business, and so bring him success and prosperity. They looked about them and came up with a candidate who fit their prescription: single, middle-aged, with a means of making a living so that she would not marry for money.

But the candidate failed in one requirement: she had a slim figure. Too skinny, so haggard, Mrs. Lee judged.

With this imperfection stated, the squad began to unearth more faults. She has that jaundiced look, one said. She'll die on her husband, the other followed. They shook their heads in concert.

Madame Françoise cleared her throat, but nonetheless betrayed some unease as she said, I have someone in mind, someone in our class.

I peeked through the slit on the bamboo door.

The matchmakers eyed each other, thinking fast. They swept a meaningful glance at their teacher. Someone in our class? Who?

Madame Françoise lowered both her gaze and voice. She's the new student.

Quickly, quickly tell us who.

Madame took her time to deliver the name.

Now, why didn't I think of it before? Mrs. Lee smacked her thigh. I sit right next to her.

She's a perfect candidate. Madame Françoise smiled.

Now that we found a candidate, it's time to tell the future mother-in-law. Mrs. Lee lowered her voice.

All the eyes turned to Madame Françoise.

What? She refused to comprehend.

Again Mrs. Lee spoke up. Teacher, since you live in the same hut with them, it'll be a lot easier for you to approach the grandmother. Don't you all agree?

It'll be a perfect match, said Madame.

Did Madame Françoise merely act under an innate impulse, enthusiastic matchmaking being a dominant trait in middle-aged women? The urge was comparable to my tirelessly walking around the camp, a way to pass the time, to distract oneself.

In the refugee camp, all of us struggled with the existential dilemma of what to do with the time. Day in and day out, this question confronted the men and women in the camp: what do I do? And what was there to do but to mill around the camp or get into disputes with the neighbors?

Or perhaps Madame was a trained Buddhist, selfless, with a big, good heart and big, good intentions, always performing kind deeds for her fellow human beings.

Or was matchmaking a method of self-defense. Wouldn't the townspeople, her students, her neighbors in the camp, gossip about her, a single woman sharing the same hut with a widower's family? Her reputation as a virtuous Ph.D., a self-respecting French scholar, might be smeared. Perhaps she was secretly hurt that none of the matchmakers made any attempt to create marriage opportunities for her. With her diploma and knowledge of French, she should be more desirable than other candidates. But everyone regarded her only as the French teacher, never as some lucky man's wife. Before the gossip started, she had to make it clear to all that she was merely a neighbor to the widower, and what would be the logical course of action? She forced herself to outdo the matchmakers at their own game.

I couldn't believe what I heard, the things the aunties said. I cared nothing for Madame Françoise's motivations. To me it was clear and simple: she was evil. Whoever planned to fix my father up was evil, a destroyer of my family.

I could no longer stay cooped up in the bedroom listening to the evil talk. I had to find something to do. I discovered the solution on one of my walks: I passed a bamboo shack, saw through the window a roomful of people sitting in rows, the classroom lighted with an eye-soothing white lamp, not with the weak giddy incandescent light.

The instructor, who probably learned his English from the Americans he used to work for during the war years, admitted me. The class met twice a week at seven o'clock and was open to all, as long as there were enough seats and students could keep up.

I enrolled in English 1300, the most advanced class that I dared to take. At the end of my first class the instructor announced that there would be a grammar test the next session.

After dinner Ahma went to visit her friends. In twenty minutes I would have a grammar test. Just as I prepared to leave for my class, Madame's new student came in. She took a seat in the second row. She was not one of the people from the old town. I had not noticed her before. It must have been her third or fourth session in the adult class.

She looked like she was in her mid or late thirties, not overweight or bony, not tall or short, not beautiful or ugly. Although average in those regards, she had a most enviable nose, uncharacteristic of typically flat Asian noses, and—I would later find out—two rows of perfect white teeth.

I wouldn't have noticed the woman had I not seen a half-secretive, half-prankish smile forming on Madame Françoise's lips as Madame stole across the living-room-as-classroom to look for my father. By the door, she frantically waved and gestured to him. His hair newly dyed black, he padded toward her with a wondering look. She stood on tiptoe next to him, cupped her hand around his ear and whispered, and then energetically pointed to the living-room-turned-classroom.

Madame's candidate opened her exercise book to go over her notes. I doubted if she could concentrate: surely she had caught the hoarse whisper of Madame and couldn't help feeling pleased to be so alluded to, conscious that a man's eyes were on her now, studying her, circling about her, but embarrassed that her teacher didn't bother to show more discretion. Correspondingly, every move of this candidate was purposeful, highly self-conscious.

A few more students arrived. My father couldn't utter anything but smiled, obliged to lend his attention to our kind neighbor.

I had to get to my own class, and stepped out casually, so as to appear ignorant of the design.

When I arrived a few minutes later at the thatched-roof classroom with unpaved dirt floor, the class had already begun, the instructor writing the test on the board.

The ten-minute test required the class to turn declarative statements into interrogatives, using present and past tenses. We graded our own tests. I missed five questions out of ten. Got confused about *do*s and *did*s. I vowed to do better next time.

My father and I had arranged to meet after class at the coffee shop, between Barracks 12 and 13, on the main street that enclosed the athletic field. As I waited for him there, I ordered a glass of hot soybean drink. Warm light spilled from the shop onto the main street, while the athletic field remained enclosed in the cool dark. It was easy to see the crescent moon. The street on the opposite side of the field shared the warm light that spilled from the shops at the front of the barracks in the twenties. The glass of hot soybean drink in front of me sent up a waft of steam, through which I saw Mrs. Lee with her squad of matchmakers emerging from the half-lit alley.

Giddy from the two-hour contact with Madame Françoise's mind, the rapid fire of her voice still resounding in their ears, the squad of matchmakers shuffled along with notebooks in hand. They took the path that cut through the athletic field to the other side of the camp, where they lived. I didn't see the candidate in the group. Perhaps Madame Françoise had detained her, or a man had taken her home—on another route, for a private moment together.

The light in the coffee shop went off. Closing time. I was the only customer left. I ordered a pair of "oily sticks" to go with the soybean drink. Tearing the doughnuts in halves, I recalled the origin of the name "Kwai oily sticks" as I dipped one in the steamy soybean drink. The oily sticks were husband and wife, traitors bound together in ropes. In Chinese history, according to the belief of the general population of the Song Dynasty, Chin Kwai, the military strategist, had betrayed the dynasty's General Zouai Fe, a hero beloved by the people, who was unstoppable, performing one military feat after another. Envious of his success, Chin Kwai set the hero up and had him killed. The populace captured the traitor, tied his wife and him up, and executed them both. To further vent their hatred and fury, the populace made doughnuts according to the shape of the pair of traitors tied together, deep-fried them in a large wok of burning oil, and served them with a bowl of steamy soybean drink.

As I drank up the last mouthful, I heard someone playing a guitar, sweet sound trickling out of the guitarist's nimble fingers, accompanied by his own slow moody singing. A magnetic voice. From somewhere nearby a woman's light laughter burst out, probably because a man whispered sweet words in her ear, his breath tickling the root of her ear, her soft white neck. The crescent moon hung low in the sky. The shop owner-waiter lit the oil lamp and then proceeded to close the shop: he put the benches on top of the tables, with the legs of the benches facing up.

Ahma was already asleep next to me when I heard the door to the hut open. I knew it was my father returning. He opened the bedroom door and stepped up into the room, making the bamboo floor creak even as he tried his best to be furtive, unbeknownst to anyone. He got inside the mosquito net a moment later and lay down. A moment after that I heard him snore.

A CRACK IN THE SKY

One evening, after the night class was over, Madame Françoise came to knock at the bedroom door. I was keeping Ahma company. As I opened the door, Madame smiled and said that she wanted me to meet someone. I stared at her. She said, Come chat with the auntie. Before I made any move, a woman came to the bedroom door and inquired about Ahma's health. Ahma said she was merely resting, and returned the greeting. The candidate spoke pleasantly.

Thinking that one day the candidate could become my stepmother, I tried to appear diplomatic. I stepped forward. And with Madame nudging my side with her elbow and darting eye signals at me, I joined the candidate in the common room.

Madame went to erase the chalkboard and then conveniently disappeared into her bedroom.

Through our talk I found out that the candidate had a younger sister imprisoned in Bangkok, whose uncertain situation made her worried. When will the Thai release her? She sighed. The candidate's sister was the only survivor in a group that were shot by the Thai at the border.

This detail gave me a jolt. I touched my forehead to feel a bump that was no longer there. I said nothing.

The candidate needed someone who knew Thai to write to her sister.

Why Thai? I asked.

They only allow letters written in Thai. They have to inspect them, the candidate said.

His Thai is excellent. I turned as I heard Madame's voice. She poked her head through her bedroom door.

You can write Thai? The candidate looked pleasantly surprised.

The boy is the perfect candidate to write letters for you, Madame told the candidate through the doorway. He taught himself Thai.

In actuality, I had learned Thai at a school in the Ubon Lao Refugee Camp.

As if to allay the fears I had not expressed, the candidate assured me she had no intention of getting married until she resettled in Canada or France. Currently she had no interest in men.

I remained still.

The Thai inspect all the letters sent to the prison, she then said. And so far I can't send any letters to her because I can't find anyone who knows how to write Thai.

I remained unmoved.

I have not written to her for two months. And then she lost her voice. She took out a handkerchief to wipe her eyes.

Don't worry. The boy will help you, Madame said, and then went on to cite an idiom for my benefit: Helping people builds the foundation for happiness.

After a look at Madame, who claimed to have my happiness in mind, and a look at the candidate, who appeared pitiful and beseeching and hopeless, I could do nothing but take out paper and pen. I said I could try, upon which the candidate broke into a smile, with tears still sparkling in her eyes. After

I wrote the first letter, my first line of defense would have been breached.

She wiped her nose with the handkerchief, apologized for it, and as she said she wouldn't know how to thank me, tears quickly flooded to her eyes again. I looked away. She tucked away the damp handkerchief and began the dictation.

I asked her if I should write in the first person, assuming the voice of the big sister. And she nodded in the affirmative. So I asked the prisoner if she needed money and clothes, asking whether the Thai would release her soon, adding that I was worried about her and would go to see her if I could. I read the letter back to the candidate and she, sucking her breath, nodded most gratefully.

She peered at her wristwatch and uttered a cry of surprise. Close to ten o'clock. She apologized with embarrassment. Before leaving, she asked me if Ahma was already asleep.

Ahma was in fact still up, lying in the bedroom. I placed the candle on the floor, in the direction of Ahma but a distance from the mosquito net. The lambency of the white candle revealed the front of the mosquito net and part of what was inside it: the pillow, Ahma's gray hair, the blanket that covered Ahma. Remaining in darkness were the suitcases along the walls, and the top of the mosquito net, and the thatched roof above it, and the sky above the thatched roof.

As the candidate came to the door, she urged Ahma not to get up, saying that she only came to thank Ahma for my help. Sitting in the doorway on the stilted floor, she then inquired after Ahma. In the mosquito net, Ahma heaved a feeble sigh. She said the doctor had told her to keep her mind calm and avoid anything that might raise her blood pressure. And when Ahma inquired after her, the candidate also heaved a feeble sigh. She mentioned her sister's situation, which was why she had asked me to write the letter. Somehow the topic that was on everyone's mind came up, and the candidate made her position clear by saying that she had no plan to get married because so far she had not found the right man. This statement should relieve Ahma's mind.

That night I slept straight though nine contented hours, without a single nightmare. Helping people was indeed the foundation on which a sound sleep, if not happiness, was based, and a good night's sleep was all I asked for. In the back of my mind, however, lurked the suspicion that the candidate's position contributed no less to the soundness of my sleep.

The candidate returned again and again to dictate to me. I translated her words, letter after letter, writing in the first person, with the same message. With the same result, for the Thai continued to hold the sister in prison.

Over time I came to know what she would say, and would draft the letter without her even having to dictate. Which meant she had less occasion for applying the well-used handkerchief to her eyes. Because tears no longer sparkled in her eyes as she smiled at the same time, I noticed her teeth, which were long and skull white. Her smile gave me shivers, the bared sharp white teeth, as if I were in an old, unlit, deserted castle, wandering into a high-ceilinged room full of cobwebs and dust, and suddenly coming upon a row of lighted white candles swinging right and left in midair. The candidate's spectral smile had that effect on me.

When she had no letter for me to write, the candidate told me about her plans to go to Canada or France. We sat across from each other at the table. She stayed late, usually until the light went off and I had to light a candle. She had become more like a friend. I called her Auntie Lan.

But as late as she stayed, rarely was my father in. Once, near ten-thirty, he came in and saw Auntie Lan and me still sitting at the table, a lighted candle between us. Auntie Lan immediately got up to leave, gathering her notebooks and checking her watch and saying with deep embarrassment that she had forgotten the time, and then thanking me for my help.

The more she spoke and rushed, her eyes jumping from the floor to my father and the door, the more apparent it became that she, caught waiting for my father, was trying to explain herself.

My father showed no interest in Auntie Lan. To save face, she repeated to me and to her classmates and Madame that she had no plan to get married, not until she resettled in Canada or France. Once, sitting at the table in the living-room area, she gave this same speech while my father was in the bedroom. The pack of matchmakers argued that a husband might be just what she needed. He might provide her with a shoulder to lean on when her sister's bleak future distressed her.

But was it possible to get married in the camp even if she felt the need to, even if she was willing? Auntie Lan countered. She had applied to go to Canada and France. If she married, she would need to adjust her plan. Would she pass up the chance to leave the camp at the earliest opportunity? What if her husband had applied to go to Australia instead? And what about her sister? Marriage was out of the question.

I spent many late nights writing letters for Auntie Lan, and always slept soundly afterward. But one afternoon, trouble returned.

I was in the bedroom and I heard Ahma talking to Father. She nagged him to get married, but didn't mention anyone in particular. He shouted, Stop meddling in my affairs.

What had gotten into her, hatching such a plot? I could think of no other explanation than that her dotage must be indulged by a new daughter-in-law. I was afraid to move, in case my movement would cause the floor of bamboo wickerwork to creak.

Because Ahma was irritating, my father became irritated. And when he was irritated, he tended to raise his voice. Even as I listened, unseen and without them knowing, I flinched when I heard his voice, even when I was not the object of his rage. His voice immobilized me, put fear in my mind.

The voice elicited a different reaction in Ahma: she cried. She tended to cry these days, her eyes often swollen red, past consolation. I couldn't tell whether his hollering stunned her into tears, or whether it was his disobedience, or her need for a daughter-in-law (the loss of one and the lack of a new one), or whether the tears were already in her eyes and would over-flow anyway and anytime, whether or not her son yelled at her, or refused her wish.

I couldn't tell what type of reaction her crying had on my father either, except to provoke him some more. On me, her crying had no effect, for I was troubled to learn that she was already thinking about replacing my mother.

My father yelled at Ahma, and she cried and yelled back at him. Then he walked off.

Ahma returned to the bedroom. I ignored her.

That night, past midnight, I lay wide-awake between Ahma and Father, troubled by the fragility of the one and the shifti-ness of the other. My elementary-school textbooks had con-tained lessons on steadiness of purpose and feelings, and loyalty, lessons to abide by.

It was the last time, it turned out, that Ahma urged my fa-ther to get married. It marked a turning point, after which her attitude underwent a change.

The next couple of weeks went by without any further out-bursts of argument. As usual, the periodic announcement woke me up at five or six. The broadcaster hurried those who hadn't gotten to leave two days earlier to get ready again for departure, by quickly gathering in front of the administration building. He read out a list of names. When he read out mine, it made me once again momentarily disoriented. Then he read out a last name, and an address, which were different from mine. I slept on.

*   *   *

The March morning threatened to rain, the sky inky gray. I went to the stall at the front alley for breakfast.

I ordered the usual: a glass of sweetened hot soybean drink with a fried doughnut. I returned to the hut after breakfast. Looks like there'll be a storm, I told Ahma as I stepped in. She sat by the mattress folding her clothes and looking sulky. They're fixing your father up with a woman, she said. If he finds a wife, we'll move out. She put the folded clothes in a suitcase.

Lately she had behaved this way. She fretted about my father, criticized Madame Françoise. Madame Françoise listened quietly—perhaps out of respect for elders—but what she heard must have grated on her ears. So when Ahma saw my father step into the hut, she chided him for wanting to get married so soon.

How do you know what I think? he yelled.

Why don't I? You're already so blatant. I know what you think: you want to get rid of me.

Nonsense.

She threw a sideways glare at him. Where have you gone at late night, hmm?

No answer from my father.

Your stepmother will starve you. Ahma turned to me. She'll starve you.

Why blab nonsense? My father hollered madly. He burst out of the door.

Ahma slammed the suitcase and announced, Get me some poison. Get me some poison! I'll finish myself off, crying that my father had fallen for a fat woman. I knew if Ahma weren't upset, she wouldn't have insulted Auntie Lan by calling her fat.

It was now my turn to comfort Ahma—just as, back in Laos, she used to tell me to hush and cajole me, gently, into quieting down after my father had given me a spanking. I stood by the bedroom door, uncomfortable with my role as a peacemaker. I couldn't leave Ahma alone. I struggled for some words to console her. I could tell her Auntie Lan didn't plan to marry anyone until she moved abroad. With her sister imprisoned in Bangkok, she was in no mood to get married.

Aware of Madame Françoise's design, my father probably tried to avoid Auntie Lan. The matchmakers got on his nerves. Auntie Lan's remaining late after her class must have caused my father to stay out, for he began to return to the hut later and later. And if Ahma had not nagged so much, maybe he wouldn't have stayed out either. Sometimes Ahma's nagging annoyed me, and I too felt like running and staying away from the hut, from the confinement of the bedroom in which Ahma lay resting and nagging, with the students droning after Madame Françoise a few steps away. My father too, just like me, needed a place to go to, a place to station his body. I became speechless.

Someone stepped into the living-room area. Anyone home? he asked in a pleasant voice.

Ahma looked up. Why you keep coming here?

The cheerful visitor caught Ahma's teary red eyes. He said he came to see if we'd made the decision.

What decision?

The TV. You can try it for ten days free, as promised. Ahma scowled at the hopeful salesman. You always want to sell us TV. She stepped toward him. I stepped aside.

Please have compassion for this father who's just lost his daughter. We need money badly. He began to plead, putting his palms together. Try it for ten days. Just ten days.

We're not buying any TV!

My daughter just died—

How dare you! Ahma shrieked. She grabbed a stick in a corner and lashed the man. Get out. Get out.

The man darted, raising his hands to protect his head. He dropped to the floor and crouched by the door, covering his face, sobbing, while Ahma stood a few feet away, panting and scowling. I pulled her hand and half dragged her to the bedroom.

After she lay down, I went to the door. The salesman had gone.

My father didn't return for lunch. Ahma told me to reheat the mackerels and have them with rice. She spent the afternoon lying down, and got up only when it was dinnertime. She reheated the mackerels and the wintermelon soup from the night before. I sat at the table. I heard the wind knock down trash barrels on the roadside and send an empty can clattering. She told me to get a bowl and the chopsticks. She put the dish of mackerels and the bowl of soup on the table, and returned to the bedroom.

Won't Ahma have some? I asked.

Ahma's not hungry. She sounded weak.

I lit a candle and put it on the table. As I ate, a bluster of wind heaved against the corrugated tin wall behind me. The candle flickered. I tasted some soup. It was quickly cooling. The door swung forward and backward, creaking. Mrs. Lee's son appeared at the door. He poked his head in. My mother wants to know if there's a class tonight, he said. I glanced at Madame Françoise's bedroom: unlighted. No class, class canceled, I said. The child darted off. I took a bite of the mackerel. The wind blew out the candle. I tried to relight it. The wind blew out the match. I left the box of matches aside and returned to dinner. The wind blew past me. I put the dishes away in the kitchen, wiped the table, went into the bedroom. Lightning. It was too fleeting for me to see Ahma inside the mosquito net. A rumble of thunder. More lightning and thunder.

As the gust lifted the outer layer of the thatches and tore away one-third of the roof, the rain poured in on the mosquito net, on the blankets, the mattress, the pillows, the suitcases, and on the notebooks beside the mattress. And as the rain poured in, my father hastened in. He immediately ducked into the corner to unhook the mosquito net as Ahma, lying in the net, scrambled up. He then rolled the mattress aside with pillows and blankets still in the net, clearing a space in the center of the bedroom. Then he pulled over a stool and put it there. He stepped on it and fought to grab the thatches, about to be yanked away any second now. As he tied the thatches one by one back to the roof with a bamboo string, the straws at the tail end of the thatches beat about crazily, while the thatches themselves flapped up and down, up and down.

I stood by the stool holding a flashlight for him and watching him repair the roof, by then a crack in the sky. The straws, shaking and beating about, on the thatches on the outer edge of the roof, reminded me of Ahma's silver-gray hair. The hair that must have stood erect the day she had gone to the Mekong to search for the bodies.

Ahma placed two chamber pots on the bamboo floor to catch the rain. With the wind shrieking above us, she asked me if I was wet. I touched my elbows and knees, and said no. She cautioned me not to get wet, or else I would catch cold. Put on some more clothes, she said.

The next morning, lying on the mattress in the bedroom, Ahma told me to go to the temple and have a monk read the sutra for my mother, this day being the thirtieth day of the month. I nodded.

If Ahma feels well, she continued, Ahma would cook something for your mom and sister, and bring it to the temple—but to light some joss sticks is still the same—that'll have to do. She sighed, hardly audible.

The cloudy sky promised more rain. Last night's storm had turned the roads into a bed of sticky, slippery mud. I went to the temple near the market, the only temple in the camp. It was built with sturdy poles, with a straw-thatched roof and a cement floor. The walls, fencelike, were woven with pliant bamboo strips.

A ceremony was in progress inside the temple—the devoted, heads bowed in reverence, knelt on the mat and chanted the sutra after a master monk who sat cross-legged on a higher tier. I looked in from the outside; I didn't have enough courage to step in because I didn't know what to say to the monk or how to request a service and whom I should talk to. Suppose I stepped in and shuffled on my knees to the master and explained what I had gone there for, thereby interrupting the monk's chant, an impossible thing to do in front of so many people, and rude. Yet I could not walk away. Hearing the chants, I thought of my mother and my sister and the service due to them. I turned away. Unnoticed.

Back in the hut, I reported to Ahma in the living-room area. She had gotten up, washing rice.

I couldn't find any monks. There was a ceremony going on and I didn't know what to do.

Then let it be so, she said. It's the intent that counts. What's in your heart.

I felt easier, yet still thought of my mother and my sister having no service done for them. The picture of them wandering by themselves looking for food tormented me.

Madame Françoise bounded in. I have some *tumsom* for the boy. It's not too spicy. He'll like it. She handed a tin plate of raw papaya salad to Ahma.

Ahma got to her feet and dried her hands with a piece of cloth. That's very kind of you, Madame. We can't let you spend money on—

It's freshly made. The boy will like it.

You have such good heart. Ahma smiled as she took the plate.

Have some now. Madame waved at me.

I stared at her. Her eyelids fluttered. She had something to hide. Behind what she said lay a different meaning. I covered the plate with a tin bowl, to protect it from flies, and put it on the table. I went into the bedroom, pulled the door halfway closed.

From behind the door I saw Madame Françoise sit on the bench two feet from the kitchen.

As you know, the boy's father, he needs a wife. She spoke watchfully. I wouldn't bring this matter up if it's any other women. But I know of one who'll be a good match. She's single, with good facial features. Madame Françoise, watching Ahma step into the kitchen, kept on, I can't stress enough the importance of a woman's face. In it is the map of her future married life.

Ahma sat on the stool intently fanning the stove and—no doubt—frowning.

A woman in her middle age, and still without a husband, has to have survival skills. Madame Françoise droned on. It sounded dangerously like she was talking about herself. It's the first thing a man should look for in a wife. Very important, she said.

However, survival skills had not attracted any suitors to her door.

As to the looks, the boy's father can decide for himself, she said.

I heard the coals crackle. Ahma kept fanning the stove; her hand must be trembling, the coals glowing.

She's somewhat on the heavy side, Madame Françoise talked on. That only means she'll have a comfortable life. And her good life is possible only when her husband has one. Now you see what it means for the boy's father?

I heard a crash of pots and pans. I rushed from the bedroom to the kitchen and saw Ahma crumpled on the floor, her face drained of color and eyes dead-fish blank. Madame stood over her.

Ahma, what's the matter? Answer me. I turned her face to one side. She couldn't speak and didn't seem to see me. She seemed paralyzed. I faced Madame. What did you do to her? You—

Madame Françoise preempted me with a raised hand, Quick, quick, get her to the hospital.

THE WAKE

In the temple, Mrs. Lee told the visitors kneeling around the coffin about her dream. It happened when I took an early-afternoon nap, she said. An old woman knocked at my door. I asked who it was. She said she came to bid farewell. I woke up, couldn't figure out who the granny was until I got the news an hour later. I should have known.

Madame Françoise, kneeling next to Mrs. Lee, said aloud, The grandson should shave his head because Ahma would have wanted her only grandson to do so—to release her from the sea of bitterness.

Madame Françoise's eyes fixed on the townspeople around her. And to save her from the pit of suffering, she said, and followed her admonishment with a sigh, audibly stricken with grief, making me feel that not to obey Madame Françoise's word would be to condemn Ahma to more suffering.

I glanced at Madame: earlier, in the hut, I would have jumped and pounded on her, if my father had not grabbed my elbow and pulled me away from the murderer's door. I stamped my feet, demanding the murderer to return a life for a life. My father hushed me and told me to use reason and self-restraint.

Now, in front of so many uncles and aunts, I couldn't say no to them. Their tongues were sharper than knives. But I didn't want to shave my head either and go around the camp bald-headed, teased by my peers. Besides, Madame Françoise was hardly the one to decide what to do and what not to do. I kept my eyes on the coffin and remained silent.

Madame Françoise brought up the subject again. Mrs. Lee nodded her vote, as did other family friends. Auntie Lan kept quiet.

I lifted my head and turned a glance at my father sitting cross-legged near the coffin. To my relief he shook his head, and said that despite one's sense of duty, driven to it though one was, the circumstance could not permit such formality. He did not believe in any of the old rites: all nonsense to him. He agreed to the ceremony, but would go no further. Also, he knew that if he said yes, other people would have taken the matter into their own hands. Already some insisted that I shave my head right away and enter a period of monkhood.

Madame Françoise was the loudest. To perform only what is due, according to the Buddhist tradition.

And it's the proper way since Ahma was Buddhist, Mrs. Lee chimed in.

Already so disobedient! The coffin has been barely closed, Madame commented.

I regarded them with dismay. But neither of them dared propose that my father shave his head, because if he did, the matchmaking would have to stop.

Another inspiration struck Madame, whose belief in demons normally was stronger than her faith in Buddha. She looked up, eyes brightened with divine inspiration, and informed us all of Ahma's last wish, to have her ashes spread on the earth.

A few others, budding oracles themselves, ventured to suggest burial. In keeping with the tradition, they said in concert.

My father would have none of the fuss. Although he appeared to listen to all guidance offered, at the end he would do only what needed to be done, and do it in as simple, efficient a way as allowable, without conferring with the well-meaning townspeople. He raised his hand for attention before he said, As I've said, the circumstance does not allow such formality.

While I felt relieved and grateful for my father's intervention and decisiveness, the thought of not doing what Ahma would have wished disturbed me.

In the midst of all the talk, the monks arrived in a file. As the chorus of matchmakers watched the monks filing in, a general hush fell on them. The monks, refraining from eye contact with anyone, sat down cross-legged on the upper tier, in a row, with the master monk in the middle. After they were seated, the monks began to recite the sutra. Each of them knelt around the coffin, palms together, head bowed. After a while the chanting slowed down, and the master monk opened his eyes.

In the crowd Mrs. Lee's husband passed me an eye signal. Taking the cue, I shuffled on my knees to the front, and somewhat to the side, of the monk. I leaned forward to offer my wrist. The master monk chanted as he tied the white cotton strings around my wrists, right then left. While the monk tied the strings, I kept my head down and listened to the chant. This was what I should have done that day I tried to look for a monk to do the service for my mother and sister. My father did not go up to the monk to have his wrists tied for blessedness.

After the ceremony the townspeople—including Auntie Lan—and the matchmakers sat around. Some chatted. I was not sure how many would sit through the night, to keep Ahma company till dawn. My friends came by. They stood around while I knelt with the visitors, to tend to the call of duty. Mrs. Lee saw her son standing by the wall. She got to her feet and moved through the crowd to him. I smelled hair spray. A few moments later she came back, and as she made her way through the visitors back to her spot, I smelled hair spray again and then I heard a whisper, I don't want him to catch the staleness of ill luck. I could sense a pair of eyes send a signal to someone behind me. When I looked around at the wall where some curious children loitered, Mrs. Lee's son had gone.

Around eleven or so Mrs. Lee's husband told me to go back to the hut to sleep. I asked, Ought I not sit through the night as well? He shook his head. Uncle'll be here all night, he said, patting his chest twice, together with other grown-ups. Now go, go to sleep. He motioned me to leave. My father too told me to go to sleep.

As I moved to the exit, I saw a stranger in white mourning attire, probably in her mid-thirties, somewhat on the heavy side, sitting in a corner among the townspeople. Who was she, this stranger in white? Could she be another candidate the matchmakers brought along? I took another look at her. But she kept her head bowed low. I walked out of the temple.

No sooner did the cremation take place than the zealous activity of the matchmakers came to a halt. None of them breathed a word about any matchmaking.

ENGLISH OR FRENCH

Madame Françoise would provide meals for us, an arrangement my father made with her. He paid her for the groceries, she would do the cooking, and we would eat together.

Eating with other family? I didn't understand why he chose to combine our household with Madame Françoise's, after what she had done to Ahma. He seemed to hold no grudges, no anger, no resentment, the way I did. Not only did he make no remonstration against having the living room turned into a classroom, not only did he accept it, live with it, he also took one step further so as to make the situation more alienating—for me.

Did he approach Madame, or did she offer to cook meals for us, out of the goodness of her heart—out of pity?

Having learned the past-progressive and present-perfect tenses, I advanced from English 1300 to English 1400. I now learned active and passive voices.

The instructor introduced an example of passive voice: was bought. A young woman said she thought the verb following "was" always ended with "ing," why was it "bought" and not "buying"?

The instructor chuckled. That's why you have more to learn, he said. There are many ways a sentence can change.

The young woman had just had her final emigration interview, and would leave for Australia any day now. She would not have enough time to learn the passive voice.

On my way to class, someone threw a cigarette butt at me. I stared at him. He stared at me. He was the thug type, mean looking, with a smug, belligerent attitude. To avoid trouble, I walked on.

The instructor emphasized drills, and often called on students. Tonight's drill, he reiterated, has to do with changing the verb form. He gave the first example on the board. Do not change the subject, he added.

The first student he called on was a young woman who had the good fortune to emigrate to Australia soon. She went up to the chalkboard and rewrote the example. THE PATIENTS WAS HELPED BY THE MEDICINE LAST WEEK.

The instructor asked the class whether the sentence was correct. A boy immediately raised his hand and, upon the consent of the instructor, left his seat and hurried to the chalkboard, picked up a piece of chalk, and hastened to rewrite the sentence as the young woman returned to her seat. He changed "patients" to "patient" and changed the verb: THE PATIENT WERE HELPED BY THE MEDICINE LAST WEEK.

The class burst out laughing. The boy too giggled along as he returned to his seat, his face flushed from the consciousness of his blunder. The young woman watched on, gratified by the instant karmic retribution. As he sat down, she stuck out her tongue and made a face at him.

I didn't feel like laughing. After class where could I go? I didn't want to go back to the hut, to be near Madame. I would take my usual long walk. It would be best not to return to the hut. Going to America would be my way out of this. I could work part-time and study part-time. I could wash dishes. I would leave my father—remove myself from his influence, from his arrangements, and start a new life. So now what I could do was to learn as much English as I could. But my thirst for knowledge had not reached its peak: out of twenty-four hours, I put in only two hours of study. I wanted to see friends, to go play. How would I spend the Saturday? My daily activities included going to class, eating, washing myself in the evening. Such a life was dry. Besides learning English, there was nothing else for me to do.

The instructor called my name, asking me to write a sentence in passive voice. I went up to the chalkboard and, after a moment of thought, wrote, HE BOUGHT HER ORANGES AND BISCUITS BECAUSE HE WAS AWED BY HER. Without waiting for the instructor to check the sentence, I dropped the chalk and returned to my seat. Unaccountably, my face flushed. "He" was awed because Madame Françoise had a Ph.D., an expert in French. Why else would "he" still keep up the appearance of neighborly harmony? I had not seen my father give anyone else such things as oranges and biscuits.

I took many classes: the formalized English 900 series, and the American English 1300, 1400 series. The instructor in the afternoon class tended to be absent. I had seen students play hooky. It was unheard of that teachers engage in such a practice. Clearly the old rules no longer applied.

I didn't study much in the daytime. Would I learn to play guitar, to become a silversmith, or learn judo?

Father said he wanted me to learn how to fix radios. The idea did not appeal to me. Why would I listen to him, obey his words? Should I take up fixing radios just because he wanted me to? I had not decided what profession I wanted to go into. A stenographer, an engineer, a scientist, a doctor?

I had a premonition that very likely I would fail at learning how to fix radios. It was a matter of interest. But how would I know if I didn't try? At least it was something new to do, something fresh.

The vocational school near the market would be open soon. I could go there to learn how to fix radios, make pastries, use the typewriter.

In the front yard of the vocational school, workmen put up decorations. They had set up a row of lightbulbs—purple, blue, and bright pink—along the new barbed-wire fence. Rolls of colored papers—pink red, orange, green—attached to a bamboo trunk in the middle of the yard stretching out, forming a circle billowing around the bamboo trunk, leading to the central hall, where the band would play. Sewing machines, typewriters, broken radios, and various pieces of equipment would arrive on the following Monday, after the celebration of the grand opening.

After dinner, I washed myself. I changed into a pair of pants, an oversized shirt. The sky had turned dark.

I headed for the vocational school to watch the celebration.

From the roadside, I looked in to see what was going on, who showed up for the dance, how people dressed up, and whether I could sneak in. The band had arrived, drums and other instruments were being set up. The shining light in the central hall heralded the festivity to come.

It was not yet eight. I went for another walk around the camp. When I passed the vocational school again, the celebration still had not started. I decided to return to the hut. Once in the hut I lighted a candle. I played with the candle wax and finally blew out the candle. The wax congealed on my fingertip. When it was near my bedtime, I decided to go find out whether the celebration had started.

Already I could hear music, the band warming up. I raced to the fence. Already there were spectators: those who didn't buy the tickets for the dance stood outside the barbed-wire fence watching. I walked around the fence to the side where it was dark.

Young men and women in Adidas T-shirts and Wrangler jeans and jean jackets bought with the money sent from their relatives abroad, in Canada, Austria, France, and the United States, packed the yard. Under the multicolored streamers, couples and groups stood talking. Some danced, swaying with the music.

I leaned closer to the fence. Had someone happened to see me, he would have thought I was a ghost stationed by the post, with arms crossed over my chest, a fence ghost keeping an eye on him, to make sure he would not misbehave.

I heard some gruff laughter, which came from the man in army fatigues standing by the entrance, one hand holding a can of beer, the other holding a woman's waist. A few soldiers were on the dance floor: they were not soldiers anymore, but wore the soldier's outfit out of habit and nostalgia, and because of the sense of power and manhood it made them feel. Or they could be freedom fighters, who did not wear the soldier's fatigues to make a fashion statement.

A woman in the traditional formal dress held a mike in her hand and began to sing a popular Thai song, "The Debts of Love." Rather than staying on the stage with the band, she took a few steps forward to be with the audience, and sang as she wove through them. The steps of the dancers swayed with her as she communicated her passion through her young, sincere, artless voice. She advised the young men and young women to treasure the youthful season, not to squander it, but to incur romantic debts.

A tall soldier was on the dance floor, with a woman in his arms, his large hands around her slim waist, a gun attached to his belt. The woman leaned her head on his chest. Her black hair coiled around one side of her shoulder and down. Her bright yellow blouse and her dark gold sarong, a gold shimmer, clung to her figure. They swayed with the music.

I knew the woman. In Laos, she was like everyone else: unadorned, untouched, down to earth. She had to drop out of school after the death of her father, to take up a clandestine occupation to support her family. My father, so I heard, had given her some assistance after her father's funeral. My father, having assisted a few families in difficulty, had developed a kind of reputation for philanthropy in town. That was how I came to know the girl, and be proud of my father. At some point, my father's assistance stopped and the girl continued her nighttime occupation. She continued the same trade in the camp. Her appearance automatically gave one the impression of debauchery and depravity. When I saw her, I knew what she did for a living. She wore heavy makeup and large heavy earrings. She typically favored wanton-looking short skirts rather than the heavy, modest sarong that she now wore at the celebration, the sarong that covered the entire length of the legs and fell past the ankles, all the way to the floor. Her hair was natural, soft, black, and long enough to glide past her waist.

The young, artless singer concluded her advisory love song, placed the mike back at the stand, and withdrew from the stage. I watched the couple, the woman in particular, to see what she was up to.

And then the tune the band had started drew my attention. A familiar tune. A popular tune. A melancholy, nostalgic tune. The song the jukeboxes in the camp never tired of playing. The man who would now sing it was not the person who sent the song across the Mekong. He brought the mike to his lower lip while he slowly raised his right hand, up and up, and then he paused. He then dropped his right hand slowly as he began in a low, mournful voice.

The whispers and giggles stopped. The dancing stopped. The flirting stopped. The smoking and drinking stopped. All stood listening, thinking of their loved ones, of their old home, of their country. My mother drifted along the Mekong, her back facing up, toward the sky.

*   *   *

My father told Madame Françoise that due to my studies this past year in the camp, I could converse with Americans. It was far from the truth, but I decided to let him say what he wanted.

Did Madame Françoise feel a sting of jealousy, a stifling wave of displeasure, combined with a choking attack of annoyance, as my father bragged to her about my progress in English? She had tried to recruit me to take her class and study French. But English was more popular, more widely used.

I knew I had made some progress. When I first started, I couldn't spot a verb or tell the subject of a sentence. Now I could recognize and use the past-perfect tense and passive voice. But I had never spoken to an American.

There was a new student in the class. He had been there for less than a week and already the teacher praised him, said he spoke good English. From the way he dressed, I couldn't tell that he was Hmong—until he spoke in that language. He often asked questions and asked them loudly. I had the impression that he liked to show off.

There was an old man in the class. It was the fourth session and yet he still couldn't tell the difference between active voice and passive voice. His eyes reddened. Tears appeared but didn't drop down his cheeks. A grown man—he was about forty—would not cry so easily in more dire, desperate circumstances. He would certainly not cry in a classroom.

While the instructor gave the lecture, the man kept shaking his head and sighing, ready to give up. The class seemed unable to help. When I encountered a hardship, who would come to my aid? I too would sigh and shake my head.

The young woman left for Australia. She sent a photo of herself with a few kangaroos in the background. She had a contented smile. Far from the confinement of the camp. She said she had an Australian name: Birdie.

Good evening, everyone. I stood in front of the class introducing myself. I said a few things about myself which I couldn't make head or tail of. I laughed. The class laughed too. The laughter closed the distance between us.

The first question for me was, Had you dinner?

Yes I had.

What dishes do you like?

How refreshing and joyful it was to be able to speak in another tongue. I vowed to study harder.

The class was over. I felt good about my language ability. Then I saw Mrs. Lee's son pass by, the boy who poked his head through the door that stormy evening. Just like that time before, he asked me if the class was canceled. I said I didn't know. He saw students walking out of the classroom, so he asked me what I was taking. English 1400, I answered, with some pride, because soon I would advance to the next level. I asked how he found French.

Learning a language was by far the driest topic. He grumbled about how hard French was. But one day you will go to France, I said. He said he would rather go to America. He had seen Disneyland in the movies, and Superman in the comic books. I want to meet Superman, he said. So why don't you take up English? I suggested. Superman speaks English.

The next morning, Mrs. Lee's son swaggered into the living-room-cum-classroom to announce to the class that he was going to a different instructor to learn English. The announcement surprised the class. His buddies were especially stirred by the news of his quitting, protesting that if he quit, they would follow him.

The boy turned to go. But Madame Françoise ordered him to sit down. He stood still, telling her again that he was quitting.

Does your mother know about this? Madame asked with a severe frown.

Mrs. Lee's son yelled, shaking his fist in the air, that he would rather learn English. He would go to America to see Superman. To the mortal terror of Madame Françoise, the other youngsters began to clamor that they too wanted to learn English, to go to America to see Superman.

Quiet! Quiet! Madame hit the ruler on the chalkboard. But the banging failed to hush, failed to intimidate, failed to bring order.

Let's go to an English class, Mrs. Lee's son yelled.

Let's all go. The monkeys jumped up from their seats.

The girls stayed seated and watched.

The monkeys snatched the notebooks off the table, pushed pens and pencils into their pockets, turned their butts, and headed out.

Her complexion ashen, her speech momentarily fragmented, her livelihood permanently endangered. Madame fought to keep her lips from trembling. Quiet down! Her command came out as a hoarse plea.

My English class was canceled again and I reluctantly returned to the hut—just in time to hear Madame Françoise in her adult night class make reference to the insulting incident.

With a sigh, Madame said she was disappointed in Mrs. Lee, whose son would not have turned out to be such a monster if she had spent more time cultivating his temperament rather than her hair, which was graying anyway. It was the parents' fault when a child behaved so rudely toward—here Madame became so stirred she had to pause to keep her voice calm—toward a teacher.

Mrs. Lee's face turned scarlet. Not even her hairdo could save her face now. I am going to discipline that monkey as soon as I get home tonight, cried Mrs. Lee indignantly. Madame, when my boy is naughty and disobedient, discipline him. Let your slapping hands fall on him. Spank his behind, Madame. You have my full permission, cried Mrs. Lee, to punish that brat.

After class Auntie Lan quickly got out of the hut, as if she had the foreknowledge of trouble brewing, and wisely stayed out of the way.

Mrs. Lee, in her seat, still looked scarlet, her bosom heaving visibly, embarrassment and shame written all over her forehead.

Madame stopped erasing the chalkboard. With a sigh, she turned to Mrs. Lee. I didn't mean to slight you in front of the class. Maybe I was heavy-handed, but it was for your sake. He will be out of control when he gets just a little older. Imagine that.

That monkey needs a spanking badly. I am going to punish him, cried Mrs. Lee.

I am sorry about having slighted you.

Oh, no, no, Madame, no. It was my fault for allowing him to be so unruly. Punish him, Madame, when he misbehaves in class. Treat my son as the son you would have. Mrs. Lee burst out with tears.

The tears solidified whatever bond they had between them.

The next day, a few kids trickled in. They dropped their notebooks on the table, slouched in the benches, the better to stare blankly at the chalkboard. Some began to yawn. Yet Madame did not correct their attitude, did not make them sit straight.

By the end of the week, all the kids who quit had returned.

No doubt still shaken by the scene of the kids walking out on her, Madame appeared meek and tamed. She reviewed the lessons, went through the oral drills, conducting the class with the conviction that she could no longer count on the young generation to make a living.

She went to the market, talked to the mothers, encouraged

them to learn French. Memory problem? Too old to learn a new language? Nonsense. I promise I will teach you. She patted their hands.

After dinner, the mothers began to stream in. Whoever wanted to learn French Madame admitted. The mothers packed the classroom, making French overtake English as a more popular language—and in the process providing an abundant supply of food for the mosquitoes.

Madame did, however, turn down a young woman, the one with long hair past her waist, the one with the night job. On a Sunday morning, she came to inquire about the class, her heavy high heels knocking lightly on the cement floor as she headed to the still-sleepy-eyed Madame who sat slouched in the doorway, her hair undone, the sarong she wore unlaundered, her teeth unbrushed. Madame said the classes were filled, and would say no more to the unexpected visitor.

Later in the morning, after she had brushed her teeth and washed the sleepiness off her eyes, Madame made some remarks in whispers to my father about the woman's visit. Upon which he said, You can't judge a person by her occupation, but by her character. Shaking her head, Madame commented, Wearing makeup and perfume in the morning!—thus taking a firm stance on the woman's character.

I was surprised too by the woman. Women in her line of work slept past noon and remained dormant and inert, hidden from broad daylight, until nighttime, when they appeared in heavy makeup once more, and became active. Yet this woman, at least on that morning, was already up and about.

The number of the adult students in the night class increased steadily. The classroom, filled to capacity, became the place where mothers and aunties gathered after dinner.

One night Madame asked the adult class how would they like the idea of having a larger classroom. A larger classroom would create a more comfortable learning environment, the class agreed. No doubt about it, Madame concurred, making it sound like it was the students' idea and she was merely seconding the motion.

She asked for donations. Everybody contributes a little, just a little, she said with warm enthusiasm, putting herself in the position of a public servant.

The invitation extended to my father the following day. She proposed that he buy the adjacent hut, to make it more like a home for the boy. She appended the proposal by calling him Big Brother, an appellation that had the effect of making a man instantly straighten his back, expand his chest, become tall, gallant, and protective.

A "little contribution" became a real-estate acquisition. But if she had counted on his gallantry before and succeeded, she would soon learn to count on it less, because this time the feminine appeal produced no result. He gave her no response.

SULFUR

My father took me downtown, to the bank. He took a piece of jewelry from the safety-deposit box. He took me to a jewelry shop. He sold the jewelry. It dawned on me that we had no income, only expenses.

I went out for breakfast around seven-thirty. I usually had porridge, which cost two bahts. It was within my budget, and the most I was willing to pay. Any other indulgence would cause me to exceed my allowance, and I would have to ask my father for money. I itemized my spending every day. Although my father did not keep the fact that we had only expenses, with no income, from me, I didn't understand its import, the shadow it cast on a person's spirits. True, I got upset about the living situation, felt unhappy, fretted, but not because I was worried that we had only expenses and no income, that the savings would run out like rice pouring through the hole of a sack. At that time such a prospect did not have the impact on me that it must have had on my father.

After breakfast, I returned to the hut. Madame had gone to

the market. She didn't ask me to go with her. Nor did I offer to accompany her, to help her carry the basket of groceries. And when she returned with the basket, a light one, I didn't help her carry it either. I thought I should, out of courtesy, offer to carry. But I had no inclination to be on good terms with her, to promote harmony, to go out of my way to get along. Nor did I get in line for the three or four salted mackerels rationed out to each household, or rush to the well when water was released to fight for water. At mealtimes I refused to make small talk. I suffered and seethed and bristled, rejecting the eating arrangements and the merger of the households even as I ate the very food that Madame had fixed. Nor did I, after each meal, help wash dishes. I persisted in being headstrong and stony, willfully refusing to play into my father's scheme.

My father did not help out with the chores either, except to get water. He could carry two full buckets of water from the well to the hut.

In the beginning, Madame made two dishes and a pot of soup for lunch and dinner. Sometimes she didn't go to the market, but simply used the food from the ration—a few salted mackerels or half of a tough, scrawny old chicken, some cabbages.

In the hut, I found an open letter behind the mirror. In the following months I found several such letters addressed to my father: a couple from France, another from Australia. I recognized the names, my father's friends. They were quite dear to me, those uncles and aunts who came to visit us in our home in Laos. Their children and I used to play together. The correspondents gave identical messages, that they lacked the wherewithal, that they themselves had difficulty making ends meet.

I forced two bowls of rice down my stomach, just so that my father wouldn't comment on how thin I was becoming.

Usually I ate only a bowl of rice. I had never eaten so little before. Even Auntie Lan said I was way too thin. I knew I would continue to get thin, because I lacked an appetite. I willed myself to eat less, to shrink the appetite to the size of a grain of rice. I preferred to skip meals, a liberating alternative, and take another walk. I let my feet carry me, trudging through alley after dark alley, past dinnertime, past seven o'clock when the night class started, past nine o'clock when the night class ended.

My father asked me to pay a visit to Mr. Lee, to collect a debt. I was put in a difficult situation. I had never done anything like this.

I knocked on the door. I hoped Mrs. Lee was out. It was the uncle who opened the door. I greeted him. He smiled and asked me to come in. Look at you, you're growing, he said heartily. I braced myself and told him what I had come here for. He said he was waiting for his daughter in Japan to send him some money. He had sent her to Japan to work.

When I stepped out the door five minutes later, my hands and pockets were as empty as when I stepped in. I told my father Uncle Lee had no money.

Madame began to skip her trip to the market for groceries. For lunch, she simply ordered some slices of fried pork lung from a hawker and served them with sticky rice and a small bowl of garlic-and-chili sauce.

My hunch was that my father had cut down on the grocery money, having learned that if he gave her more, she would ask for still more. Judging from the low quality of the meals, he had even come to suspect that she pocketed some of the grocery money. He reduced the sum, or had even skipped a payment or two, which made Madame less inclined to fix a proper meal.

My father would look disgruntled and eat in silence. He ate

little, and finished lunch quickly, and stepped out, leaving me
to finish it either by myself or with Madame Françoise. I knew
my father preferred meat and eggs. Ahma had always included at least one meat dish for a meal, but Madame had replaced this with fried pork lung, which was not to my taste,
nor to my father's. He began to miss lunch. Sometimes
Madame Françoise would eat in her bedroom, and I ended up
eating by myself in the living-room-as-classroom.

What do you complain about? Who does the cooking?
Madame Françoise sat in the doorway of her bedroom, her
knees spread apart in the sarong she wore. In Laotian, her
scolding lacked an object, almost as if she scolded herself. Did
she think she was alone? Screaming so openly exactly because
no one was around.

She went on. So picky. Buy yourself ten kilos of beef. You
want seafood? Think you're a king? I cook every day and you
show up, eat, then walk out. Do you think this is a hotel? My
place here?

It was getting dark. I stayed still in the hut: any movement
would cause the bamboo mat to creak, and Madame would
know that I was in the hut and had heard all she'd said. Perhaps she knew I was in here, and it bothered me that she,
whether or not she knew I or my father heard her, would go
all the way so recklessly and "rip faces." Perhaps because she
didn't know I was in the hut, she felt free to rip faces. My ears
spicy hot, I had no defense.

Her face and ours at stake, Madame Françoise kept on
scolding. Did I keep the money? Did I keep the grocery
money? Come and check my pockets then. Come. She had
drawn up one leg and leaned against the doorway. She didn't
care that my father might step into the hut at any moment for
dinner. She did not cook dinner. She dared him to walk in. If
she used only part of the money for food, of course my father
would cut off the payments, or withhold them until she used

up the money for groceries. Because he stopped paying her and had the audacity not to show up for lunch at all, Madame had to "bite" him first.

A few feet from her: the benches in the classroom, the dining table, the posts, the door blended into the growing darkness. So did everything in the bedroom I stayed in: the luggage, the pillows, the blankets. Holding my breath, I heard the volume of Madame's voice wear off with the heat. The sun, round and red, and seemingly flat, must have been slowly sinking behind the trees in the distant field outside the barbed-wire fence of the camp. The buzz of a mosquito drew near. The perpetual curse landed on my leg. I didn't dare to slap it even as I felt the itchy sting.

At last I heard Madame step out of the hut, the sound of each step alternating with my pulse, until eventually my pulse was the only sound I heard. She had left—instead of dinner, "torn faces" on the table. Suppose my father, on his way to the hut, ran into her in the alley?

As I fumbled for a candle in a corner of the room, I told myself I would get a job as soon as I landed in America. Just as soon as I got out of this camp. I read that many foreign students in New York worked like cows and horses in restaurants. I could do that too, work like a cow, labor like a horse.

My breathing became uneven. I waited a moment before I slipped out. I shuffled along the alley between Barracks 13 and 14, from the end of the alley to the front. When I reached the front alley, I turned left to the main road, passed Barracks 13, 12, 11, in decreasing order, on one side of the road and the athletic field on the other. When I reached Barrack 3, I turned right. I went to the coffeehouse, where I assumed I would find my father.

Peeking in, I saw instead a crowd cheering and yelling in front of a black-and-white television set. A football game? I made my way to the counter and asked the waiter, an acquaintance, if he had seen my father. No, he had not.

Where else? I stood outside the coffeehouse looking right and left. People milled past me. There were only so many places one could go to. I went from barrack to barrack, around the athletic field. I passed by what used to be a cemetery— now replaced by two rows of barracks. So, the administration had achieved two purposes: not only to remove the coffins from the marshy place (and put them in a dry place, I hoped), but also to build barracks on the site to accommodate the increasing number of arriving refugees. The new residents on the former graveyard heard the dead sob at night.

As I hurried along, sweating now, I caught the stern eyes of an old woman.

She stood by the roadside holding a cane with both hands and chewing betel nut with great jaw movements and studying me. I took a look at her.

Why do you follow me? She scowled, her voice harsh.

The question puzzled me, so I looked at her.

She drew back, to the edge of the gutter, and spoke. Why do you follow me, huh?

I'm not following you.

What do you call this? You're following me just now. I've seen you before, all over the place. So who are you? Get away from me, do you hear? Get away! She swung her cane to chase me away. I know it's you. Don't let me see you again, I warn you.

I drew away from her, to avoid contact with the cane, in case she was a leper, her cane contagious with the germ of leprosy.

Shortly after I had blended into the endlessly milling crowd and walked along, I saw a figure in a familiar gray-white shirt and dark pants appear ahead, shuffling toward me but not seeing me. I couldn't tell where my father was coming from or going to. Where had he been? I moved toward him and breathlessly blurted out what Madame had said about us.

No, she was talking about somebody else, my father said. You heard it wrong.

She lied about us, I said.

You misunderstand.

She scolded us, I said. You weren't there. You didn't know. To convince him, I added, Ask the neighbors, then. They heard it. She said we let her do all the work.

My father said, She's the fire coming to us, we are the water going to her. She was pointing the arrow at someone else, not at us.

I was unconvinced. Certainly Madame, whose mind I had misread, did not point the arrow at Mrs. Lee. So I said, Of course it's Mrs. Lee, that long-tongue. I saw her whisper something to Madame. She gossiped about us, and Madame believed her.

My father shook his head, smiling, as if amused by the gossip.

The time to split the stove is now, Papa. You've misjudged Madame. Now that we know her true colors, we can cook separately. We don't have to depend on her.

He merely nodded, said nothing was the matter, and told me to go back to the hut to sleep. He asked if I had had dinner. We went into a noodle shop nearby, and he ordered only a dish of chow mein. He said he already had dinner. Where? As I ate, he told me to go to sleep after I finished the noodles.

Don't worry. Nothing is the matter. Don't think about it, huh?

I nodded. My eyes began to tear. I wouldn't have to put up with so much if I had a home. I kept eating until not a strand remained on the plate.

We walked for some distance afterward, before he told me again to go to sleep. We parted in front of a barrack on the main street. I turned around to watch the figure in the gray-white shirt and dark pants heading in the opposite direction. Where was he going? After I lost sight of him, I headed back to the hut. All the lights in the alleys had gone off. I shuffled through the alley to its end, where the hut stood.

I went in. In the bedroom, I shone the flashlight on my watch—almost eleven—and switched it off. I spread out the mattress and the mosquito net, hooked the net's ends onto the four corners of the bedroom, lifted the net, and crawled into it. I removed my watch and placed it by the pillow. I judged from the stillness that Madame's hut was empty. Past eleven, yet she had not returned. The watch ticked.

I couldn't sleep. My affection and respect for my elders had lulled me into believing that they were loyal, decent people. I remembered Madame taking me to the Café Français as a kind gesture, and Mrs. Lee fondly teasing my sister, likening her to a Japanese doll, as clear as if it happened only yesterday. How had all that turned into sulfur? I fell into a troubled sleep.

Sometime during my troubled sleep, I smelled alcohol and heard my father snore. It was uncharacteristic of him, to sleep like a drunk.

I went to the market the next morning, heading straight for Mrs. Lee's stand. She sat on a low stool, behind the stack of cigarette packs and mosquito coils and toilet paper, ready for a customer.

As I approached the stand, I fought to keep calm. I then cried out, There's a snake!

It startled her. Snake? Where?

I crossed my arms with a smirk and walked up. It's hiding here, in front of me, I said.

Mrs. Lee looked ill-pleased.

Oh? I caught the snake, so let's not beat about the bush. I crammed a hard edge in my voice. You know what you did.

What? What did I do?

Don't you pretend. You know very well what happened. I tried to sound nonchalant, knowing that to be effective I needed to balance the hard edge in my voice with calmness. What did you tell her? I saw you say something to her.

Who?

Who? I was incredulous, dropping my arms. Madame Ph.D., your French master! That's who!

We were just talking, you know, grown-up talk.

Actress, I sneered. Why do you act like a thief if you didn't gossip about my father, huh? Why is she upset, then?

How would I know? And what does it have to do with me? Don't make things out of nothing, child. Stay out of it!

I don't make things up, unlike you. I saw you. It's you. I pointed at her.

I am not on anyone's side.

I don't need you to be on my side. I want the truth. What exactly did you say to her?

Stay away from grown-up business.

You bad-mouthed us.

Everything I've said about your father is true—

So now you admit you said something. Again I sneered, refolded my arms. Who's the one making up things?

Child—the forked long-tongue's voice turned sharp and loud—don't think your father is such a holy man. Your grandmother has barely lain down in the grave and now he has found a woman—during the mourning period!

Auntie Lan had assured me she had no intent to marry, and I didn't see anything between her and my father. I took a deep breath and glanced at Mrs. Lee. You make it up, I said.

Everyone knows what kind of a person your father is.

I began to snap, I'm not talking about him. I'm talking about you. With you spreading rumors like this, of course everyone knows.

You think he's so pious.

That's not the point. Why else would Madame act up like that if not for you? You troublemaker. Don't deny it. I know what you've done. And don't you tell me what my father is like. I stomped away.

Mrs. Lee yelled, Open your eyes. Ask around. He goes to

see a woman at night, eats with her. Not only that, he goes around complaining about Madame Françoise's cooking. That's the kind of person your father is. Now he has a woman cooking for him.

Other vendors along the aisle peeked from their stalls.

I left the market. I knew my father disliked eating sticky rice and fried pork lung all the time. He gave Madame the money for groceries; why didn't she get some decent food?

Around ten p.m., Madame let out a shriek. Snake! She burst from her bedroom, gathering the bottom of her sarong as she stumbled down the steps. There is a snake in my bed! She screamed some more, shuddering.

In our bedroom, my father was about to rush to her bedroom to check, but when he got up I pulled his arms to stop him. Father, I am scared! And I screamed up his ears. I'm scared.

I could care less how many snakes were in her bed.

It is not rainy season yet, my father muttered, snakes are already out.

We have to get some sulfur, Father, I said.

Madame sat shuddering on the bench.

Madame, why don't you go in to check if it's still there? I suggested, holding on to my father's hand.

She wouldn't go in.

Did you touch it? How large was it? I bet you it's gone by now, I said. Good night, Madame.

The next day I went to the market to buy some sulfur. I spread the sulfur powder around the hut, both outside and inside, and in the corners, and around the kitchen and the bathing area. Where the walls and the floor met, there was a yellow line of sulfur to guard off the further advance of snakes.

* * *

For lunch, Madame steamed the sticky rice and made the raw papaya salad and a meat dish with beef. My father stayed around. Madame put the food on the table and, smiling and soft-spoken, told us to eat first. I sat down with my father and we ate without talking. I found the food hard to swallow.

THE INTERVIEW

We had another emigration interview in January, an auspicious start for 1980. After this I would simply wait for our names to appear on the departure list. I would join my aunt in America and leave all the nuisance in the camp far, far behind—now that I knew why my father stayed out so late and why the matchmakers stopped blabbing and campaigning for candidates, the hushed mouths of the matchmakers forming a conspiracy against me. Because Auntie Lan was more concerned about resettling abroad than about hunting for a husband, Madame or Mrs. Lee shifted her target and secretly, and successfully, fixed my father up with another woman. Madame's initial campaign to have me befriend Auntie Lan also worked to Madame's advantage, since my friendship with Auntie Lan misled me into believing that Madame had stopped playing the matchmaker. But beginning with the day we left the camp, my father would have to stop seeing whoever Mrs. Lee said he had gone to see at night. The lovers would have to part. I would split the stove with Madame for good. My father and I would then have our own home in America and wouldn't have to put up with any outsiders.

I washed myself, scrubbed my toenails clean, wore the gray khaki pants, the white shirt, in order to appear neat and proper. My father too wore a white shirt and gray khaki pants.

We waited for our turn outside the interview hall, situated by the edge of the dusty athletic field on one side, across from the stilted one-story administration building on the other. Crisscrossed wooden bars made up the walls, so that the interior was visible from outside. A large crowd gathered outside the hall.

My father registered our names at the entrance and we stood waiting. I moved through the crowd to peek in. In the middle of the large high-ceilinged hall stood a table. Behind it sat a large *farang,* the American interviewer. A dark-skinned Lao man sat next to him. Across from the table, in front of the two men, sat a family, short, thin, and dark-skinned.

Because of the size of the hall—the tall ceiling, all the empty space—even the *farang* looked small. So did the table. Most of the interviews took half an hour, while a few took only ten minutes. When the person at the entrance called our names, we walked in and moved toward the center.

After we sat down, the Lao man at the table verified our names. The interviewer spoke to the dark Laotian man while eyeing me steadily. The Laotian translated for us.

He was born in Laos, my father told the translator. He lived there all his life. He could speak, read, and write Lao very well.

The translator turned to the listening interviewer for an exchange of words. Mr. Interviewer says he—the translator pointed at me while addressing my father—isn't dark enough. He looks more like a Vietnamese—is he Vietnamese?

My throat felt dry. I should have listened to my father and gone to the football field every day so I could turn sweaty and dark like the people gathering outside the hall peeking in, and like the children running and chasing each other in the thick dust of the athletic field, with faces grimy, shirt buttons missing, shorts torn in the back, barefoot, what my grandmother called "ill-bred and barbaric."

No, my father answered, he is not Vietnamese. He was born in Laos, in Luang Prabang. He lived there all his life, speaks Lao, reads and writes the language.

Ask him if the boy is his son, said the interviewer, his eyes fixed on the two refugees sitting across from him. Those blue eyes looking at my father were transparent yet mysterious and inscrutable.

Yes, he is my son, my father answered the translator.

The translator turned to the interviewer and mumbled something. The interviewer, with a slight frown, appeared thoughtful. Then he jotted something down and proceeded to other questions which my father answered in a straightforward manner.

This Karen—is she your real sister?

Yes, he and his sponsor Karen were brother and sister.

How do you prove it?

They had the same parents.

Is it the truth?

Yes, the same parents. Same father, same mother.

"Sane father, sane mother"? the interviewer raised his eyebrows at the translator. What does he mean by "sane father, sane mother"?

Their parents are the saint, the translator said.

The interviewer frowned, then asked slowly, word by word. Do you mean "the same"? He had to make sure my father's word matched the information on Karen's petition from the States. He turned to the translator. Tell them they have to be straightforward—do you know what I mean by "straightforward"? They have to be honest, okay? It's very important to be honest in their answers.

The translator nodded.

Something spilled out during the interview. Perhaps to find out if we had conflicting accounts, the interviewer asked me about how I came to Thailand. My father and I exchanged glances, for he had not asked me anything of that nature. I didn't know if he had read the letter I wrote to my mother, so I doubted if he knew what I went through, even though he had dispatched an escort to get me. Now he would learn something about me, as I was put on the spot.

I said, One afternoon some friends and I biked to the Mekong River. My hair a nest of heat and sweat—

Even as the translator did his best to relay my meaning, the interviewer put up the universal stop sign with his hand. Could you tell the kid to restrict his account to the facts, please. I am not interested in poetic descriptions of his hair.

My face colored. Either I had said something wrong or something had been changed during the translation.

Tell him to cut to the chase, said the interviewer.

"Cut to the chase"? The translator turned to the interviewer with an uncomprehending look.

Then, as the interviewer gazed down at the paperwork, he broke into a chuckle, shaking his head in seeming amusement. He said, I have a list of refugees to interview and I'd better cut to the chase myself. Save the description for some other time. Just tell what happened.

So I said after I reached the shore, the Thai patrol guards pointed their rifles at me, swinging the weapons this way and that way across my face. They screamed at me, threatened to shoot me. I was aware of my father watching me and I found it difficult to talk. My nerves jangled. I took one step back, to the side of the guard post, and attempted to talk reason with my voice and hands trembling. The guards pulled my hands while I tried to free myself and cried for mercy. One guard looked mad. His hands reached the rifle but I tried to grab it and our hands became entangled. He tried to pluck my hands loose but I would not let him and kept crying for mercy after

mercy. They put me in jail, and I bit my lips and could not continue in front of my father anymore, leaving the translator to
talk.

After we left the interview hall, I felt light and free. The
cathartic release that came with my confession somehow
made me feel closer to my father, who had not told me anything at all about my mother. Silence on the subject, in turn,
made it difficult for me to talk to him. Nor did he ask anything
about my experience of swimming to Thailand. I didn't volunteer the information either—until the interview.

This is what happened: The group of us fumbled up the
shore. We waited until all of us climbed ashore. An older boy
spotted a flight of stairs the size of a dragon's spine arching
upward to what looked like an outpost, on the riverbank. At
the base of the spine, we stopped for breath, and panted. I
shook my head at the earth a few times, to shake water off my
hair, and I took my shirt out of the plastic bag. Our stomping
up the stairs of the sentry post must have woken up the two
coast guards there. A moment later we looked up to find ourselves at gunpoint.

The guards advanced toward us with their rifles pointing.
The face of one guard contorted with rage. His hands reached
for the rifle when they became entangled with my and my
friends' hands. The hilt of the rifle hit my forehead.

The guards locked us up in a detention center without light
or food. In the dark cell, frightened and hungry, I tried not to
think about the mistake I'd made, to feel sorry for having un-
dertaken the crossing, which had seemed courageous and
promising, and which, in hindsight, seemed so reckless and
ill-advised. The mosquitoes kept us company, and stung us.
The buzz kept us awake while the bites of the night before
drew more mosquitoes each subsequent night.

One morning, a guard came to the cell. Why didn't they put
us in the refugee camp in Nongkhai, our intended destination?

The guards, whose faces always looked twisted with foul temper, hollered and pushed us. I was frightened by the hollering and the sight of the rifles. I could barely walk, let alone fight or cry. My nose runny, my arms and legs bitten and swollen red, my feet covered with blisters, like a leper—a detestable sight to the Thai guards.

I kept scratching my head in a frantic effort to gain relief from the itch. I had not had a decent shampoo for countless days, and some kind of rash had begun to spread here and there on my head. I rubbed the spot, feeling some gluey wetness on my scalp. I pulled along the length of my dirty tousle. I could smell the discharge on my fingertips.

The guards put me in a truck along with others. After almost a day's ride, I got off the truck to find myself finally at my intended destination, the refugee camp—but instead of Nongkhai, it was a place called Ubon. A guard put me in a shack. When I got hold of a pen and a piece of paper, I wrote an urgent letter to my mother. And told her what had happened to me.

Near seven in the evening, I was about to step into the hut to get my language notebook when I heard Mrs. Lee grilling my father about the interview. Because I was tempted to eavesdrop and also because it would make me uncomfortable to face Mrs. Lee after having confronted her and called her a snake, I stayed still. I took a peek and saw her feet—and a few others'—stepping on the sulfur powder that I had spread along the wall.

Mrs. Lee said to my father, They checked the facts, they contacted your sister. It won't be long, trust me, before your name gets on the departure list to go to the great America.

We still have a long waiting period, my father said.

Which, for an eager bridegroom, must feel like an eternity. She tried to suppress her laughter; the result was a teasing, slimy tone, snaking into my ears. The slimy voice continued, wriggling down my spine, I believe this separation will help bond you two more tightly, after which the speaker let out the laughter that she had tried so hard to suppress.

Vulgar woman! Traitor! I tried my utmost to control the raging impulse to charge forth and slap her face, the auntie I was taught to respect and had come to hate.

Laughter continued.

He can't wait to go to America, an auntie told the others.

You can write to her, another told my father.

I couldn't stand listening to any more of this. I went to my English-language class.

In class, I imagined myself sneering at Mrs. Lee, my eyes narrowing to contemptuous sidelong slits. My voice sounding equally contemptuous: How tightly do you think they will bond? My father would be in America while the woman remained stuck in the camp. He couldn't take her along or sponsor her over. Eventually she would have to go to whichever country admitted her. Perhaps Austria or Canada, somewhere insufferably cold. It was futile to try to concentrate on the lecture.

The next morning I went to the Hmong sector of the camp, the part of the camp strictly for the hill-tribe population, beyond the market and the slaughterhouse, beyond the dusty field.

During one of my walks there I had chanced upon a hole dug by the edge of the camp. A big hole that could, with enough rain, become a reservoir. I plodded along, and while crossing the open field to the Hmong camp I saw a pale white moon in the light blue sky. Perhaps the same moon could be seen from half the world away, in San Francisco?

I didn't see any lowland Lao on the Hmong side of the camp, unsurprising, because the lowlanders didn't usually go there. Oddly I didn't see any Hmongs either. As I trudged along I heard the wailing tune of a musical instrument that dragged on and on like a dying breath.

I looked around but saw no one. The music wheezed on, a lament that made me think of a funeral. I should probably turn back.

I had known my father would scold me after the interview, especially if I failed it. He looked grave as we left the interview hall in silence, a short reprieve for me. Then he had bellowed, I told you so many times to get out in the sun. Never listen. Now see what happened. All because of you. Make them suspect you. He pushed my head, making me stumble two steps forward.

I reached the pit. Bowl-shaped, its bottom in the shade, the hole opened before me. A few dragonflies skimmed over it, dipping up and down. A rooster or two crowed, probably from a Thai village over the field outside the barbed-wire fence. The January sun felt warm. I could slip under the barbed wire and get out if I dared. I went down the slope with careful steps, but stopped midway, because I wanted to stay away from the shade. I crouched down, testing if I could sit down on the incline. And after I had slowly eased my crouch to a sitting position, I took off my shirt and stretched out my limbs for a quick tan.

My eyes closed, I imagined myself speaking English one day, a rush of gargles pouring from my throat the way my father rinsed his mouth after brushing his teeth. That day seemed so far away I couldn't see it, the day of speaking the language as fluently and admirably as that emigration translator did. It seemed so impossible even as I memorized more vocabulary in order to make it possible.

Just then I heard the sound of pebbles rolling down the slope. I opened my eyes. She stood near the rim, leaning on the cane she held in her hand, chewing vigorously, and eyeing me sternly.

Why do you keep following me, huh? Who are you? Stop following me around. Get away from me. Get away, do you hear? Trembling because she was so worked up.

I grabbed my shirt and couldn't run away fast enough.

She limped after me, pointing the cane. Why are you following me, huh? I know it's you. You've been following me.

During the few times that I went there, a few people came to the hole. I couldn't believe it. They sat around the hole along the incline, stretched out their pale limbs, turned their faces to the sun, and, while their eyes closed, wondered if the others showed up for the same purpose, and with this thought they became even more self-conscious. It was the first time for all of us to sit still and idle under the sun for the specific purpose of turning our skin darker so our new tropical looks could be more convincing to the interviewers. Just the way they thought we should look.

Each believed that he or she had found the only secluded spot in the refugee camp to pursue this secret tanning.

I didn't get any darker after a few trips to the hole. The longer I sat in there without anything to divert me, except to hurry the sun to turn me as brown as a coconut shell, the more impatient I got. I didn't know it could take so long just to get a tan.

It was Madame who brought the good news. She cried as she darted into the hut, The list is out!—flailing her hand. She must have been one of the few to first see the list, because, indeed, next to matchmaking, there could be no greater diversion.

Of course my father and I had to see it for ourselves. We hurried to the interview hall, saw no crowd gathering outside the entrance. We made a turn and headed for the rear, where it was packed with people. We squeezed through the crowd, our eyes frantically darting on the list. Shoulders pushed shoulders. My eyes found the list, shot to the top of it, someone pushed me and my eyes fell to the bottom of the list. It dropped out of sight. Feet jostling. A push from behind made me lurch forward. The list reappeared. My eyes searched for the target, name after name, down the list. My eyes moved to another list, started over, searched. Breathless, I found my name, and my father's, fixed on the list, staring back at me.

My father handed over my sister's bracelet to the proprietor of the jewelry shop. It was the last piece. The cotton purse was empty. No more rings, necklaces, bracelets. I recognized this last piece. I had seen my sister wearing it. It was too large on her small hand. My mother liked to dress her up to look like a doll, and the bracelets on her hands made her even more doll-like as she sat primly on a low stool. So doll-like that pinching my sister's cheeks, hooking onto the dimples, became Mrs. Lee's favorite gesture when she came to visit us and saw my sister sitting on the low stool.

My father had no use for the purse, and the matronly proprietor certainly would not keep it. She must have recognized my father, the man who every now and then came to unload his jewelry. She then turned around and sold what she bought, a businessperson ready to facilitate exchanges. She had no attachment to jewelry herself.

He used the proceeds to buy me a pair of sneakers.

I then took him to a record store. I named the Thai songs I'd heard on the radio and the jukebox for the merchant to record on a cassette tape.

To make sure the merchant got the right song, I described it to him. The song about a man in Thailand singing and sending his love across the Mekong to a woman who still remained in Laos, the woman he had left behind. Both of them knew better than to count on seeing each other again. As he sang, standing at the riverbank, his farmer's pants rolled up to his knees, a body drifted near him. A bloated being, with black hair like an outgrowth of moss, matted, lifeless, uncertain as to which way to drift.

I spoke to the merchant in Thai. I didn't think my father understood it. Holding his hands behind his back, he strolled back and forth in front of the glass display, browsing through the assortment of tape recorders and radios.

The merchant told me to pick up the cassette in a few days.

My father took me to a tailor and ordered two long-sleeved shirts and two pairs of pants, to wear in America. For the shirts, I picked the black cloth with thin interweaving red stripes, the light green cloth with brown checks. For the pants, it was plain solid khaki. The tailor measured my height and my shoulders, and so on, the way my mother had done. From now on I would have to go to a tailor—to a stranger—for my clothes.

We came to the Mekong. We looked across the span of water to the opposite shore, where I hoped to see a dog running, a motorcycle going by, any sign of activity, but I saw only trees and shrubs, so wild and overgrown that they seemed to have covered the entire city of Vientiane, hiding it from sight, making it appear impenetrable.

I wrote on a piece of paper my mother's, sister's, and grandmother's names. I took the paper with me to the master monk. But I didn't light the candles, nor did I bring food. The master monk did not read out the names on the paper. This was where I bungled. I was too self-conscious to make my wishes clear.

The day before our departure, Madame Françoise threw a farewell party.

With us gone, Madame would be free to demolish the bedroom and expand the classroom to the point where her voice would become hoarse just from trying to reach the students seated at the very back. A much more accurate projection would be this: the new residents converting the classroom back to its former self, restoring the living-room area, for Madame also had a couple of emigration interviews herself, and any day now the announcer would broadcast her name at five in the morning, summoning her to the front of the camp for a better life in France.

In the meantime, at mid-morning, Madame stumbled into the hut with two six-packs. She left them on the table and hurried out, and soon returned with two parcels clutched to her bosom. A man, a pedicab driver, came in with more beers and unloaded them on the floor.

Madame enlisted a student of hers to take on the sole culinary responsibility of starting the fire, steaming the sticky rice, chopping the beef, boiling a pig liver, pounding the crispy rice in a mortar, mixing the rice powder with the meat.

One of the parcels contained meat, the other parcel "bloody clams." I was shocked by the sight of the bloody clams, a seafood item, something rarer than chickens. Their meat was red, and potent, I imagined, a rich source of iron, and therefore to find it in the camp was out of place. I was more displeased than shocked, because this was the time for frugality, and because, knowing Madame, it meant the source of this luxury was someplace other than her own pocket.

The labor came with a cost, and Madame must have generously compensated the cook. She finished making *larp* shortly before neighbors and family friends arrived at noon.

They filled the living-room area. And outside the hut, at the end of the alley, they set up chairs and stools along the ditch by the bedroom, under the thatched-straw eaves.

Madame opened the six-packs and, with a broad smile, went around handing out the beer. Each holding a bottle, the neighbors toasted my father and wished him an auspicious beginning in America.

Auntie Lan showed up. She was free to come to the hut, not necessarily for her lessons, and free of the need to explain herself, now that the matchmakers had completed their mission. Did she feel slightly jealous when the matchmakers blessed my father?

In the classroom area, an elder at the table took out some

white cotton strings from his pocket and bade me to move closer.

I sat down across from him, kept my head bowed, extended my wrist over the table, and held up the other hand, thumb and fingers aligned in front of my nose. Auntie Lan, Madame, Mrs. Lee, and others, drew near, gathering around the elder and me.

The elder brushed the string over my wrist repeatedly while chanting words of blessing and best wishes, words that would follow me to America, draw happy circumstances to me, and repel all mishaps and diseases by acting as an invisible, impregnable armor.

Auntie Lan, Mrs. Lee, and others stood shoulder touching shoulder, leaned-forward hairdo crowding hairdo, with eyes open big and unblinking, ears pricked up.

In the middle of his chant, the elder wrinkled his nose, for just then his olfactory sense was beleaguered by the smell of hair spray. Not to be overcome, he forged ahead with the chant. After he finished, the elder tied the string around my wrist. He performed the same procedure on my other wrist.

The party slowly, inevitably, reached its boiling point. *Larp* was consumed. More beers were called for. Faces became pig-liver red. Voices boisterous.

Send up your wedding invitations. Don't forget, her face red and perspiring, Mrs. Lee yelled across the room to my father among the male guests.

I look forward to going to the wedding—in America! Madame Françoise followed her own statement with a loud hiccup.

Impossible, I thought. What a joke! Once in America, an ocean away, my father would be out of their reach. Unless the woman followed him there. But America was a big country. Let her look for him!

I won't miss it even if I have to crawl to get there. Mark my word. Madame took another swig. Come, let's go toast the future groom. Her hand holding the beer bottle was not at all shaky, but her steps were.

A young man, with the top half of his tight, large-lapel shirt unbuttoned, stopped Madame with a bottle raised in his hand. Big Sister, come have a toast. He grinned, offering her the bottle. Its mouth reached toward her, waiting. Suddenly she looked flustered. She made a gesture to brush the bottle away but the young man held it steady.

I looked away from the pack of housewives and caught Auntie Lan's eyes. Why did she look at me that way, across the table? I pretended I didn't hear the matchmakers and asked Auntie Lan about her plan to go to France or Canada, whether she had found a sponsor. She had sent out the last letter I'd written for her. She was still waiting for the Thai to free her sister. As I talked to her, I thought I probably would not see her again.

She then pulled me aside, whispered to me that there was something I must know. She said she had seen Madame stepping out of a jewelry shop in downtown. Later, in the passenger truck back to the camp, Auntie Lan saw Madame sporting, just briefly, a gold bracelet. It was tight on her wrist. She put it away in her purse, overflowing with happiness. I'd heard that Madame had saved enough of the grocery money to buy a piece of jewelry for herself. The piece my father had sold. The piece found on my sister's wrist. The meal arrangements still held: my father provided Madame Françoise with the money to buy food and she did the cooking, in charge of our two daily meals until our last day in the camp.

The drinking and eating—financed by my father's sale of my sister's bracelet—and laughing went on until late afternoon.

The next morning, at five, we gathered in front of the administration building, by the flagpole. Three buses were parked along the curb. My father lifted the suitcase, holding it over his head, and handed it to a man on the roof of the bus. The man stacked all the luggage on the roof and roped it off.

Auntie Lan showed up by herself. I already felt the distance between us stretching as I watched her in the crowd—people coming to see their friends and relatives off. I didn't see Madame or Mrs. Lee.

As others began to get on the bus, my father and I followed them. I sat down next to the window. At daybreak, the driver started the engine. And Auntie Lan took out her handkerchief and generously applied it to her eyes. People waved. A Thai guard lifted the bar at the sentry post to let the buses through. The wind swept inside the bus. And soon I lost sight of the waving hands.

A fire burned down the camp ten months after I left. I heard the news from a budding entrepreneur in San Jose, California. He had just left the camp and brought with him the photos he took of the fire. According to him, some believed it was arson, while others blamed the weather and chance. It happened on New Year's Eve, he said, a windy evening, people celebrating the New Year. Somebody tipsy from drinking alcohol threw away a lighted match or a cigarette butt. The fire reduced all the barracks and all the huts to ashes. Not a single hut remained. The refugees relocated to a detention center, and the camp was never rebuilt.

The man sold the photographs, through word of mouth and mail order, to fellow refugees in the U.S. who had stayed in the same camp. I paid ten dollars for the photo. I couldn't make anything out except patches of angry red and black, and lurking dark shadows. The refugee camp had disappeared from the earth.

A GIANT CAT

To Ms. Lan
Lao Refugee Camp 32/5
Nongkhai
Thailand

Dear Auntie Lan:

At this moment I am on my way to Hong Kong. In other words, I am on the plane writing this postcard to you. You will see the front of the postcard is the very jet I am aboard. Thai Airlines. Smooth as silk. Do you think the jet is big enough or small?

I just finished eating. What I ate included a hamburger, a slice of strawberry pie, some cold cuts, some fried chicken.

The plane took off at the Bangkok airport at seven o'clock in the evening. It flew over the sky of Laos and Vietnam. Now it is fifteen minutes to nine. In about half an hour the plane will reach Hong Kong.

I took this postcard from the flight package on my seat, and, as the tide rises and ebbs, I felt like writing to you.

Take care.

March 12, 1980

It was already ten o'clock when we arrived in Hong Kong. We stayed overnight at the Singapore Hotel in Kowloon. The van took us through the tunnel full of cars.

The next morning we connected with the flight to Tokyo. The trip took five or six hours. The Tokyo sun was setting when we arrived, and yet it was drizzling at the same time.

From Tokyo we flew to Seattle.

In the jumbo jet, I saw through the window the unchanging blue, truly the convergence of the sky and the ocean. I did not invoke any deities for a safe flight—as Ahma would have liked me to. Nor did I throw up or suffer a headache or an earache. The jet did not jerk up and down, or lean precariously right and left, or squeak, as the Lao Royal propeller planes tended to do.

A broad span of brown mountain range scattered with snow came into view. My father leaned over me to take a picture. We had waited for the sight of Seattle, packed with skyscrapers. Instead we saw the rise and fall of the mountains, so close to us we felt we could sweep our hands down one slope and up the next. A long asphalt road ran alongside the mountains.

I leaned away from the window.

The jet landed at sunset. Shafts of orange sunlight slanted through the plane windows as the jet moved on the runway.

At customs, big, tall *farang*—what I had seen in foreign movies—became real. Big bodies, big heads, large faces. They wore large, thick uniforms and walked with broad strides.

In the Land of Giants, we and other fellow refugees huddled together and faithfully followed the guide—our Laotian countryman—step-by-step through the *farang* to the checkpoint. After we went through customs, the guide quickly handed out a winter jacket to each in our group. It's freezing, he said. You'll need this. The jacket had a funny hood attached, and all had the same alternate light and dark blue stripes.

So gaudy. How could I accept it? I held it in my hand. It looked new and it was free.

The group disbanded, each family going their own way, boarding planes that would take them to different states. My father and I would board the plane to Ohio, to meet our sponsor, my aunt Karen, whom I had not seen for more than ten years. Her first husband was a Caucasian, her second and the current one a Laotian. In the wall of unseeing giants, my father held my hand tightly. The plane to Ohio had not arrived yet. The guide told us to stay where we were and, when the plane arrived, to board it. Our sponsor would pick us up at the airport, the guide assured us.

Two hours later, we were on board a plane to Ohio.

In his eagerness my father forgot to keep his voice down as he talked on the phone at eleven o'clock at night.

In the next room, with no TV to divert me, I lay on a mattress trying to shut out his voice and to fall asleep by picturing snow falling, as it did outside the window. I pictured a squirrel in a burrow, its head curled into the thick fur of its tail, its eyes tightly shut in the oblivion of sleep.

My father comforted the person on the phone, Cry no longer, cry no longer. I'd never heard his voice so gentle, so glib.

From what I'd overheard, I knew there was a lonely woman who went to the movies in San Francisco Chinatown, by herself after work, and stayed there till late. I guessed back in the refugee camp she had been the cause of my father's staying out so late, after Ahma's death. Now in the States: after the movies, loneliness must have continued to prey on the woman night after night, because she dialed our number in Ohio, across half the continent. The phone talk lasted so long that it became a lullaby for me, tucked under the thick blanket.

The next morning my neck felt sore and stiff. The pillow was too big and flat. I turned around and saw a new layer of white on the windowsill. The sky had cleared. All I heard was my breathing.

After the toilet I went to the kitchen. And I would have remained there lost in thought, staring at the snow, had I not run into the largest cat I'd ever seen.

Perched on a neighbor's snow-covered deck, the cat was the height of a two-year-old child but was twice as wide, her fur a fluffy white. Her ears pricked up, she eyed me steadily. I was probably the first Asian she had ever seen—in my nightclothes—just as she was the first cat I saw after a month in America.

Ever since my arrival I had sunk into the gloom of the winter. I hardly saw any cars pass by my aunt's house. I never saw my neighbors on the block. The whole of America seemed to have been evacuated.

Ahma would have taken the sight of the giant cat as a sign of prosperity, the herald of wealth and happiness. How well fed, she would have said. How well grown. At the same sight, my sister would have giggled, skipping from the back door to the deck to pat the cat. Whereas my mother would have reacted to the cat the same way I did, eyeing each other from a distance—one indoors with arms folded tightly across her chest; the other outdoors, perched and alert.

I returned to my room and sat by the window. No sound of movement from my father's room yet. I checked my watch. The sound of a car came near. I leaned forward to look.

A car pulled into the driveway. Boots stomped down the stairs. The door closed. Aunt Karen, wrapped in a bright blue overcoat and a waist-long red scarf, stepped out. She greeted the driver, the Laotian wife of an American in the small Laotian community in town. The Laotian woman started the car. They drove away.

I waited a few minutes to make sure I heard no sound in my uncle's room. Then I went to the kitchen. I fetched a glass and opened the refrigerator, grabbed the milk carton, filled the glass half-full. I studied the chalky liquid that would make me grow, although I would prefer to heat it up and add some sugar, instead of drinking it plain and cold. I gulped down the tasteless liquid, quickly washed the glass, hurried back to my room.

About noon I heard a car for the second time. I peeked out the window but saw no vehicles. Across the street, the houses, their windows and doors, were all shut tight. Then I heard a singing voice from the next room. My father had not sung once, not since leaving Laos to look for me in Thailand.

Now, no doubt, as he tidied the mattress, straightened and folded the sheet, and got ready to brush his teeth, he sang slowly, in a pitch and tone that I'd never heard before, from him or from anyone.

He sang a poem I'd just read. About a courtesan entertaining her merry guests in the pleasure quarter by the shore of a river. Across the water, beyond the plains, lay the scene of ruin: invasions and domestic disputes had caused the downfall of the dynasty. Towns were deserted, homes smoldered, warriors lay slaughtered in the fields. It surprised me that my father knew any poems and could even sing one, the melody of it topping all songs in its curvilinear sadness.

I tiptoed to the door, opened it, and peeked out: the poetry anthology I'd left on the hall table the night before was not there.

I pictured the poet joining the procession of refugees. He did not know how long he could keep up. They had been trekking for weeks now. Blisters grew on the poet's feet. His hair and beard had grown long, dirty, and gray. If his wife had run into him, she wouldn't have recognized him.

The poet stopped for a rest by the shore. He squatted by the edge of the water to clean his face, when he heard a girlish voice singing in a distance. He looked about him. Across the river, the singer remained unseen. Just the light and happy singing over the mutely flowing water.

At sunset, the poet wandered into a large, deserted house. The dusty door was ajar. A large cobweb hung in the doorway. He stepped in, fumbled his way through the maze of cobwebs. A dust-laden table lay on its side; a torn drape dangled. All the household goods were gone. The poet stumbled into a garden where tall weeds grew through a fallen fence. The chicken coop was empty.

The poet fell asleep in the garden. In his dream, his wife combed his hair in front of the tall, oval bronze mirror. He was an officer of the court, not yet a poet. Husband and wife bantered as she combed his black hair. They blew out the candle.

The poet sat up: all pitch-dark, the night sky ablaze with stars. He noticed a twinkle and large tears rolled down his cheeks. He fumbled about him, weeping; his hands touched the earth, cold and hard as his wife's grave.

He realized he was still in the garden. No dog barked in the distance. No insect hummed nearby. Night wind rustled through the weeds.

He recalled the light and happy singing. As he imagined the singer to be a courtesan entertaining a group of court officers, two lines of seven words each came to the poet. He gave the courtesan's song a title.

It told the story of an emperor, an inveterate pleasure seeker spending all his time with his female entertainers, accompanied by an array of musical instruments. The singing was so melodious that even the goddesses in heaven could hear it. It tempted them to descend to the lower plane, just to enjoy the quotidian, humble existence of the emperor—who was ignorant of the mutiny that his henchmen were plotting. The song's title was identical to the last three words of the poem.

A car crunched through the snow and pulled into the driveway. Car doors closed, boots crunched on ice, Aunt Karen thanked the driver for the ride, the front door opened and shut.

If somebody has any sense, he'd better get out of his room and help me carry these upstairs, Karen called out in Laotian.

In my room I heard Uncle Ken hurry out of his room to the stairs to help his wife carry the groceries up.

Aunt Karen spoke in her jingling voice. What time is it already? Still sleeping? They're killing me. You know how heavy these bags are? They're not just for myself.

I cringed.

In the kitchen, after he put the groceries in the refrigerator, Uncle Ken prepared lunch. He cut two tomatoes, peeled and shredded the raw papaya, to prepare *tumsom*: sour (from lemon) and spicy (of course, from red or green chili), and salty (from fish sauce and shrimp paste), and sweet. All flavors except bitterness. Because the raw papaya was small and there was not enough of it, Uncle Ken peeled a carrot, never an ingredient in traditional *tumsom*, and shredded it.

Aunt Karen grumbled, What time is it? Almost noon. Isn't anybody hungry? I took a peek through the door: on her knees, she spread sheets of Thai newspaper in the middle of the kitchen floor where we would all gather around and where she would place bowls and spoons.

Just then my father sang again, the same poem. It traveled to my room and to the kitchen. My aunt and uncle stopped their cooking to listen, captivated by the melody. But Aunt Karen broke the spell by starting to cook, making loud noises—the *clink-clank* of spoons and bowls—to override the power of the poem.

I ought to help. If I could only make pleasant small talk with her as I helped her set up the table, instead of being so stiff, with a silence so insufferable. Because I acted awkward around my aunt, I felt my father and I had overstayed our welcome, and this only made me more awkward.

She called out, Lunch is ready.

Not only did she serve the food she'd cooked, she would have to scrape away leftovers, clean the floor, wash dishes. By then the frothing rage in her bosom would grow as large as the house.

I went to the kitchen.

My father was already seated on the floor, his legs crossed, waiting for everyone else to join him. Uncle Ken, standing by the counter, his back turned to us, put the sticky rice into the bamboo rice box while Aunt Karen, her back also turned, checked the oven.

Come sit down, my father told me.

I hesitated. But because he told me to, I sat cross-legged next to him.

Aunt Karen sat down with her legs modestly folded side-ways. All sorts of things in the market here. Beef and milk, she said, a bowl and chopsticks in her hands. Everything you want.

Uncle Ken ate with his hands. Plenty of meat. Everything you can eat, he said, chewing. Then he drew a leg up to his chest. As he swallowed, he put his hands together at his chest, slowly raised them to his forehead and looked heavenward, as if he saw something on the ceiling. Then he looked down, mumbling, Oh, thank Buddha, the camp days are over. We're starting a new life now. My aunt had never set foot in the refugee camp and her new life in the New World had begun in the mid-sixties after she married an American fighter pilot. Uncle Ken raised his hands past his forehead to heaven and stayed still for a second, to signal gratitude.

Every one of the Americans is big and tall, my father said.

They eat beef, observed Aunt Karen.

It's the milk, Uncle added. A glass of milk sat by his feet.

A grown-up drinking milk, and drinking it cold too? I re-mained still. Get some. Uncle Ken motioned me with his chin to get milk from the refrigerator. When I didn't move, he said, Don't worry about drinking it up, and in a spirit of generosity, he added, Just drink all you want. It makes you grow.

They drink milk like we drink water. Aunt Karen turned toward her husband.

I glanced at my father: by "they," did she mean the Americans or us?

Look at you—Aunt Karen pointed at her husband—drinking so much already. Do you think milk is cheap like water? You'll drink away money.

I chewed. My maternal uncle Chao in San Francisco, on a visit to Laos a decade ago, had told me about the Golden Gate Bridge and Chinatown. The orange structure, with a golden sunset in the background, the sun in the form of the round bowl in my hand, appeared before my eyes. I wondered how the Chinese there made pots of dollars from washing dishes for Americans who were too busy.

Lately, as I sat by the window in my room staring at the snow coming down in fluffs nonstop, with the subzero temperatures and night arriving at four p.m., I had been having visions of the bridge and Gold Mountain oranges.

I chewed the rice my aunt had paid for from the bowl that she would have to wash. I firmed up a decision. When I finished, I put my bowl away in the sink and went back to my room.

I heard my aunt say, He hardly talks.

My father must have set his mind on eating because he gave no answer.

She added, Boys are noisy and loud, not wordless.

Boys don't have gray hairs either, Uncle Ken said.

I was sure she gave him an admonishing look. My father kept eating, and his silence indicated to her his acquiescence to what she'd said.

This part of the country is too cold for him. He's used to the tropics, she said.

If Uncle Ken threw her a look to hush her, she would dodge it by reaching for the sticky rice with a gesture as relaxed as her voice.

He'll get used to it, Uncle Ken hastened to say. Here is his home.

If he caught the look she threw him, he would further betray his unease by turning away from her to peek at my father. My father must have had his mouth full, because he didn't say anything.

Not good shutting himself in the room all day, Aunt Karen said. Take a walk or run in the park. American kids do that. More healthful.

My father must have swallowed once and, chewing somewhat easily now, said, You're right, Sister. He needs to play some sports and he needs to open his mouth more often too, and open it louder and wider. You're right. He stands on ceremony so. It's his way. Correct him, Sis, whenever you can. Don't ever think twice. Change him.

In my room I heard no more complaints from my aunt. I sighed with relief. I didn't need others to tell me what to do, though it would be so much easier if my father ordered me to wash dishes.

I picked up the phone to call Uncle Chao in San Francisco. Two rings. A voice I recognized said hello. He asked me where I called from. Ohio? He echoed, and immediately asked me to move to California.

Someone knocked on the door. I hastily said a few more words into the phone and hung up. I opened the door. Had my aunt heard me hang up?

She must have heard my heart pounding as she crossed her arms and stepped past me into the room. It's not that cold today. Why not take a walk in the park? She smiled to herself before she faced me. Helps digestion, you know. Gets the blood circulating.

I'm fine here, I stuttered, stepping back.

She took one step forward. Come, come on, take a walk, get some fresh air. Then she smiled, seemingly to herself again. Auntie can go with you.

I know the way.

I know you do. She eyed me steadily.

I can go by myself. I know where.

Good. It'll be good for you. Don't stay cooped up in the room all day.

Let me get ready, then, I stammered, grateful for her kindness.

Why did she speak with such hardness when she could speak softly and be congenial. I had no memory of her, and when Ahma spoke of her, she did so in a tone of disapproval, for this auntie had defied Ahma's wish and married an American fighter pilot. Ahma refused to speak to her, and she moved with her husband to America. Until my arrival, I had not known she had divorced her husband and married Ken, a Lao refugee. Although she didn't show the warmth that I expected from an aunt, I told myself to be grateful, for without her serving as our sponsor, we wouldn't be in the U.S.

I put on the striped jacket handed out in the Seattle airport, slipped on the pair of sneakers my father bought in downtown Nongkhai.

As she watched me, still with her arms folded, Aunt Karen smiled.

I'm going now, I called out, at ease now that my aunt's voice and smile had warmed me.

By the staircase I saw that Aunt Karen had returned to Uncle Ken, who was washing the dishes. The toilet flushed and my father opened the bathroom door. Husband and wife exchanged a look. Uncle Ken washed his hands, dried them on a towel.

I went downstairs, opened the door, shut it behind me.

How coincidental. Just when I made my first phone call to California, my aunt had had the foresight to knock at the door. I could tell what had led to it. In the kitchen, she opened the tap to let water run over her voice before she had whispered to her husband, who stood by the sink, about to do the dishes, Make sure you tell my brother about those long-distance calls.

I know, was his obedient answer.

She gave him a sidelong look. He's going to run up the phone bill, she added, talking every night, that woman he talks to.

He just got here. He doesn't know.

Just got here? He's been here too long.

Things are still new to him—

Right. That's why you have to tell him.

I will.

Tell him phone calls cost money.

Ken stared at Karen.

You've got to do something about him, Ken.

I know, I know. Ken saw that his wife was about to speak again, and became impatient. He's your brother.

They eyed each other. Just then they saw my father heading for the bathroom. Aunt Karen leaned away from the sink, wiped her hands on a towel. She went to knock at my bedroom door.

The entire block was empty of cars and pedestrians. I crossed my arms, huddling tightly as I headed down the street toward downtown, not to the park. To keep my sneakers dry, I avoided stepping in the slush. I approached downtown fifteen minutes later—only then did I begin to see one or two cars driving by.

I went to the restaurant I'd passed a few times before. The sign was still behind the window, HELP WANTED. From my language lessons in the refugee camp I knew that meant I could go in and apply for a job. I recalled the story of the foreign students making pots of dollars from washing dishes alone. I looked in and saw a counter person and a waitress.

I walked to the end of the block and turned back, passed the store, and looked in the restaurant again. My sneakers were wet. I needed to hurry.

A familiar figure in the same kind of hood and jacket I was wearing walked down the street. He saw me and I stopped for him to come near. Then we walked on together. We passed the restaurant.

Did you have enough to eat? he asked.

Au, my way of saying yes.

He asked again if I had had enough. We could go into the restaurant and point to the food.

We walked on slowly. I thought about my decision. He too appeared thoughtful. But neither of us would say what was on our minds.

The decision took a few quick turns in my head, and stumbled out of my mouth. I've talked to Uncle Chao, I said. I looked to my father for some reaction.

My father stopped walking.

He asked us to go to San Francisco, I continued. What Uncle Chao had told me on the phone was to move—not just go—to San Francisco.

My father must have caught the eagerness in my voice and eyes, because he surprised me by saying, It might be a good idea to go out there to take a look. Then he saw that my sneakers, bought in Nongkhai from the sale of his last piece of jewelry, were wet. Look! He pointed. Hurry back quick. You'll catch cold walking in the snow with these shoes so wet. Hurry.

In the evening, as I crouched in the bathtub scrubbing the dirty sneakers that I would wear to the Old Gold Mountain, I hummed a popular song by Teresa Tang.

My father passed by the bathroom to return the poetry anthology to the lamp table. He had not heard me sing since my early school years. He knew I loved pop music, all about passion and broken hearts.

The boy wants to see his maternal uncle in the Old Gold Mountain, my father told Aunt Karen in the living room a few days later. He'd brought it up a few times already.

If so, she said calmly, you will need to book plane tickets.

Uncle Ken offered to book the tickets and, avoiding Karen's eyes, asked my father if the tickets would be round-trip. But when my father said, Your wife is right. Here is too cold for the boy, Uncle said nothing more.

Her chest heaving, Aunt Karen kept her arms crossed. I watched her walk away.

The next day my father dyed his hair in the bathroom. I found some stains in the sink and, in the trash basket, a discarded package with the picture of a woman with long brown hair.

When I saw my father, I noticed his stained fingertips, his hair youthfully black. He told me he had booked a flight.

THE SILVER PHOENIX

The plane landed at midnight. The passengers took their belongings from the overhead bins and filed through the aisle to get off. I stepped up on the armrest to get my bags, but my father gripped my arm and told me to wait until the passengers cleared the aisle.

The exit door might close at any moment and no one would know we were still in the plane, stranded there. But as always, what he told me to do, I did by reflex. Only after the aisle had nearly cleared did my father stand on tiptoe to reach the overhead bin.

As soon as the flight attendant by the exit greeted us with a smile and followed it with a rapid succession of words, I found myself already inside the brightly lit airport. Embarrassed for not understanding the flight attendant, we let our smiles speak for us.

A woman, somewhat on the heavy side, with bouncy shoulder-length hair, came toward us and I knew right away she was the woman my father talked to on the phone. I recognized her even with her makeup and modern clothing—her dark red pleated knee-length skirt and black high heels—instead of the plain blouse and the sarong and slippers I imagined she had worn in the camp. A broad forehead, lively eyes, a proper nose, full lips: the entire face lay open like a mirror. Good facial features, just as Madame Françoise would have said.

I did not step up to introduce myself, to say hi. I was trained not to butt into grown-ups' talk and not to speak until adults asked me to.

My father made no introduction either, but trusted the woman and me to figure each other out. He reasoned: in the camp I must have heard the rumor that he was seeing a woman, and in Ohio I must have heard the phone talk too. When she asked him if he needed help carrying the bags, my father hastened to decline.

As she asked him, she caught my scrutinizing eyes. But delight and a sense of excitement had taken hold of her and she didn't seem to mind.

I had not thought about what to do once we arrived in San Francisco. It had not occurred to me to call Uncle Chao again, to inform him of my arrival date and time. So when I saw the woman, I regretted my oversight, and now that I was caught in the obligation of staying with her—who knew for how long—I also felt betrayed.

While the woman probably read my facial expression as curiosity about her, my father took it for a combination of shyness and formality, for he told her I was *si-mun*.

Let's get the luggage first, she said. On the way to the baggage claim she remarked, People are free to do things here. Look at them. She motioned with her chin toward a group of five or six long-haired, sleepy-eyed hippies lying on the floor along the wall.

Free too to sit on the ground in public places? my father asked, looking askance. Right in the airport!

Isn't this too free?

I always think so, he answered.

Here it's common though. Other people don't even look at them.

Sure enough, other passersby did not seem to notice, did not so much as glance at those hippies. Casually lying around, they abandoned themselves to cards. A few were in deep, trancelike embraces, oblivious to my glance.

What I had heard about California was true: you could kiss in public and no one would care; you could lie around in public.

At the baggage claim the woman turned to my father, saying, It's going to take a while for the luggage to come in.

The other passengers from our flight were waiting around too.

The woman talked about her new name. I couldn't get used to it. Me, a black-hair, black-iris woman with a foreign name? Carol, Karen, Kelly. Shaking her head. It just doesn't go. Why bother, then? you might wonder. Then I thought, why not Lilian? It sounds like my Chinese name. Li Lian. But then people corrected the spelling and put another 'l', making it Lillian. I said no. It's not Lillian. It's Lilian.

The chute began to churn out luggage.

Ten minutes later we were on the freeway. From the car I saw trees, their dark shapes, shaking wildly with the force of the wind off the murky, roiling bay. It was the first time I had seen so much leafy green since my arrival in the States.

And so much traffic. Trails of red fireflies glowed ahead of us, while four curves of flying torchlights zoomed toward us on the other side. Bewitched by the trees along the freeway and by the traffic, which represented so much activity and wakefulness at such a late hour, I decided, right then, I would stay.

On the freeway a valley full of light came into view. Dots of light spread densely across a grid. When the traffic veered right, I saw the sign for the Golden Gate Bridge. I felt it—how would I express the sense of its closeness, its hovering presence? Just knowing it was close by made me itchy all over.

But Lilian took the lane to the Bay Bridge, a bridge I didn't know of.

After the valley of light, I began to see high-rises. Towers of lanterns, hundreds of lanterns, hailed us, waved to us, beamed at us. The warm glow of lanterns adorned a pyramid. Turning around I saw a dome, brightly lit, the roof of the city hall, as I would later learn. Islands of clouds floated there.

Moments later I found myself already at the base of the tall, cloud-piercing stupa.

This pyramid building is the landmark of San Francisco, Lilian said, pointing as she drove.

I committed it to memory.

When I saw large red signs with green words that denoted seafood and egg noodles and a blinking picture of a red swimming duck, I knew we had arrived in the Chinatown that I'd read so much about and had seen so many times in daydreams while in the refugee camp. I didn't expect to see street names in Chinese, such as Curry-Food-Near Jear, or Carry-Food-Here Street, the translations of "California Street." The streets looked so messy and filthy.

A street farther away was barricaded and all lit up, with a gathering of people. Something is going on, I observed.

Probably a movie crew, Lilian replied. This kind of thing happens all the time here.

I looked about me, for the camera.

Lilian took us to the Silver Phoenix for wonton noodles. Roast ducks hung behind the greasy counter, their long necks curved through a hook. The smeared old clock behind the cash register read 1:30. Amid the hubbub of talking diners, the waiters served tea, set out plates and bowls, bused the tables.

After we sat down, Lilian warned, Beware of the gang of the black-glove society. Beware. The gangs here are everywhere.

A matronly waitress wearing a greasy apron came to take our order, jotting it down as she blabbed out, One wonton noodle, one dumpling noodle, one roast duck noodle, and fried tofu angles? Is that right?

Lilian said, Hai, hai. After the waitress returned to the kitchen, Lilian continued, We must be very careful here. Don't ever carry cash with you. Put your money in the bank. Take out the money only as needed, a little at a time. Me, I carry twenty dollars at the most. If a pickpocket sees you wearing a gold bracelet, he'll cut off your hand.

The warning lost much of its intended effect since my father had already sold all his gold in the refugee camp. Of course, of course, he said. These days who still has gold necklaces and bracelets to wear? Who has any gold left for flaunting? No more gold to brighten under the sun.

There are fools in this world, you know. A Sacramento Lao woman wore a handful of fake rings out on the street, against all common sense. Think about it. Didn't she know that's exactly the kind of break robbers look for? She couldn't help herself. A fool. They cut off her fingers. Lilian paused for the news to take effect.

My face turned ashen, and if I spoke at that moment, my lips would have shaken. Robbery—the mention of it made me cringe—and the repeated mention of the word "fool" was jarring and upsetting. Didn't Lilian know about my family? When she was in the refugee camp, surely she must have heard about what happened. If my father had not told her, some bigmouths and long-tongues must have. I had learned to rely on gossip to spread things I found hard to talk about. So why did Lilian harp on jewelry, and robbery, and fools, and details of dismemberments? I fixed her with a resentful glance.

Yet she went on. The majestic among us will still wear jewelry. But you don't see Americans wear their gold on the street. Why? Because of the black-glove society. Americans buy cars and stereos, never jewelry, not even a fake piece.

I heard a loud voice: Have you heard about the shooting across the street here not long ago? The voice became both secretive and confiding: Gang robbery.

My face turned pale. The loud voice belonged to a woman at the next table. The people there, probably her grown children and their spouses, looked at us unblinkingly.

The matronly gang leader pointed at Lilian while eyeing my father and me. This lady is right. You have to be careful, she said, as if heckling a timid victim, her spittle flying. The person next to you can turn out to be a robber. Happens all the time. Right in Chinatown. Dangerous place. You don't know about this, do you? You just arrived? Where from? She wouldn't leave us alone.

I felt like sticking my fingers in my ears. What was taking the waitress so long to bring the noodles over?

Just then three gunshots sounded. The nosy woman shut up instantly, turning pale. Lilian turned pale also. A hush fell on the chatty Silver Phoenix.

The man behind the counter, the guardian of the cash register, stood up, raised his short, chubby hands over the diners for attention, and tried to reassure everyone with his commanding voice. Nothing to worry about. Nothing to fear.

Three more shots. Fear entered the Silver Phoenix, crashing through the glass window, and once inside, he machine-gunned everyone present.

But the guardian of cash repelled the blinding bullets of fear with his armor of prescience. Combating the terrorist not hand to hand or gun to gun but with his naked voice, he called out, Calm down. Let's calm down. It's only a movie. For those who don't know, they're shooting a gangster film in the alley behind us. He named the director. Famous action-film director. You'll see when you go to the back.

At once the Silver Phoenix returned to its boiling chatter. So it's only a movie. Scared me to death. The nosy woman patted her chest with her fist, to show her mouse heart thudding out of control. Thank heaven and earth. They shot another movie around here too. 007.

That was ten years ago! the person next to her corrected her.

At last the waitress came over with bowls of noodles. Sorry, really sorry about the false alarm. Did it frighten you? She put down the bowls of steamy soup one by one.

After the meal Lilian took us to the back alley, the one I had seen lit up with blinding lights. I couldn't tell who or where the director was as we stood behind the barricade among the onlookers. He was supposed to sit behind a big camera.

A man in a tight all-black jumpsuit, compact, slim, no doubt a movie star, charged breathlessly down the alley, away from a few other men who were chasing him; the thugs, clearly.

One thug threw a flying knife. The spiderman, or lizard-man, or ninja, or a traitor of the black-glove society, or a professional assassin did a somersault, causing long black hair to slip out from the cap, revealing the he to be a she. While still in the air she caught the flying knife and, before landing on the ground, threw it back in a flash quicker than it had come at her. The thug who had thrown the knife stopped, clutched his chest—as if hit— fell, sprawled. The lizard-ninja-assassin then began to tackle the thugs who had spread out in a closing net. She backflipped, kicked, blocked the attacks with her arms, punched, darted, turned, jabbed, blocked, somersaulted. The villains hit, got punched, got jabbed, flipped, flopped.

Why would she run in the first place if she's so good, huh? Father shook his head.

Movies, you know that. Lilian chuckled.

To deceive fools, he said.

I looked away.

It's getting late. Let's head back, Lilian said. The cocks will crow soon.

In the car my father said, They could have filmed this in Hong Kong. Why come all the way here?

Lilian laughed. Not real over there. It's more real here. The real Chinatown.

Tonight, there had been too many mouths all too ready to dispense wisdom.

I looked at the clock. Almost eleven. I got up, opened the door, tentative about my steps. Through the half-open door, I saw no one in the living room, though I could hear my father and Lilian talking. I didn't mean to eavesdrop but I heard the names of Aunt Karen and Uncle Ken. I stayed still.

Father: She shouldn't say things like that outright, never.

Lilian: She's been here too long.

Father: More than fifteen years. She's learned the American way.

Lilian: Maybe that's why.

Pause.

Father: She took it out on the poem I sang. She sent him.

Lilian, in a soft low voice, told my father not to mind Uncle Ken.

My father cried out. She was convinced I sang the poem to criticize her. She got the innuendos all figured out.

Maybe you should have told her what you thought. Americans don't keep things inside their chests. They like to talk things out.

A grunt from my father.

For us it's hard to do, I know. Lilian continued, But since Karen is Americanized like you said, it's better to be straightforward. Ask her why. Confront her. She won't think it's rude. Americans like that. They'll respect you for being rude. Try it. She'll like it. If you keep quiet, she'll think you a weakling. She'll look down on you and step on you.

My father sighed.

Lilian continued, I know it's hard. I too have problems with being frank and verbal. But once you get used to it, you won't think speaking out is rude. Then she sighed. Her voice filled with empathy, she told my father he could stay as long as he liked.

So this was what had happened on that day in Ohio, when I ran into my father downtown. After my aunt had sent me to the park, she sent her husband to have a talk with my father about our overstaying our welcome. Uncle Ken's directness offended him and Aunt Karen's craftiness angered him. My father knew he should be rational, but he felt hurt, unaware that he needed to make the necessary decision he'd put off. He had said nothing but let Uncle Ken finish what he had come to say.

Uncle Ken perhaps was more direct, his chi more fiery. My father was calm, much more able to keep down his chi, to keep his cool and his humor. As he paced, with his hands held behind his back, the cloud of an idea began to hover in his head. As he continued pacing, the cloud condensed. He put on his striped airport jacket, went downstairs, slipped into the pair of snow boots that Uncle Ken had given him.

By the time my father stood outdoors sucking in icy air through his mouth, the cloud had congealed into a plan, a solution. He shuffled headlong down the street, toward downtown. The only pedestrian on the block, he wasn't sure how long he could take the snow, this permanent freezer.

He thought of Lilian. On the phone she had told him about San Francisco, It doesn't snow here. The weather is warm almost all year, very suitable for us Asians. This is the place to settle. This thought was in his head when he saw me down the street.

Now, in Lilian's apartment, I closed the door and tiptoed back to bed; and in case my father came in, I climbed into bed and pulled the blanket up to my chin and closed my eyes. I then smelled the odor of the blanket, foreign and unpleasant. I opened my eyes and held my breath for a moment. My stomach growled.

The talk in the kitchen seemed to have ended, and sure

enough, soon afterward my father came in. He said, Time to get up. Auntie Lilian has the day planned for us.

I turned over, throwing my arm to one side. I rubbed my eyes and yawned.

Come, get up. We'll go places, he prompted.

Half an hour later we all got in the car. As soon as I sat down in the back, I smelled its stuffiness, another foreign odor. And when Lilian got in, I caught a light scent from her in the driver seat. What kind of perfume did she use?

It began to drizzle as Lilian started the car. Drops on the windows blurred my view.

We passed Golden Gate Park.

The largest park in the Old Gold Mountain, Lilian the tour guide said.

Rain shot down on the tall trees. I recognized the trees although I saw them for the first time. I knew the word "eucalyptus," from the cover of a romance novel I'd seen, the transliteration and the drawing of a tall tree. Rain slanted down on the trees and the clearing far below, where a group of women practiced tai chi with a white-bearded Asian master in an all-black outfit.

I rolled down the window. The traffic moved fast although there were lots of cars.

That? It's a radio tower or TV station. Forgot its name. On a clear day it looks like that tower in Paris. I guess every city has a tower, Lilian said, noticing me looking at the Sutro Tower. Only the tip-top shows through the clouds. What is it if not a ship in the sky?

Thick clouds gathered below the top of the tower.

I played mute, unfriendly to my hostess. I should have said a few words, instead of appearing like a country boy who had never seen a big city, hunched in the backseat.

My father came to my rescue by talking to Lilian. He put in a few words in response to hers, and she continued talking.

In the obscurity of the backseat, I abandoned myself to the

view. As I watched trees, buildings, and cars, I heard my father. TV every day? he told Lilian. What a harm to schoolwork. For him—pointing his head my way—no TV. No stereo. Kids here are spoiled.

I glanced at him sideways.

Lilian said, You can't spank them either. It's against the law to discipline children by flogging. Police can arrest you.

Democracy, he grunted.

You can only talk to them gently, guestlike. You can't force them to do things they don't want to do.

He sighed.

His pompous air and tone annoyed me. I shifted in my seat, and became conscious that the car was the hostess's. And she did the driving as well. I had come to San Francisco to see my uncle, not to be with this stranger whom I felt obliged to please. If only I could go to places on my own, instead of tagging along with my father, who tagged along after the hostess.

Just then, I saw the tip-top of an orange structure looming beyond the trees and immediately recognized the Golden Gate Bridge. Such a dull orange. Just the top edge, the view was partial, incomplete. A fleeting view. It did not excite me as I thought it would.

This is the parking situation on weekends, Lilian explained, back in Chinatown thirty minutes later.

We were on Washington Street waiting to get to the underground parking lot on Kearny Street, below the park where seagulls and pigeons fluttered and shit on the chessboards of old people who came there to play. Drivers honked at the bovine movement of the cars ahead of them.

A woman on a pair of roller skates shot past the cars. Down the hilly street! And with such speed! Unhindered by the pedestrians, the traffic, the steepness of the hill, and the wheels spinning under her feet. In a few seconds she was already two blocks ahead of us. She continued undeterred.

I remembered from its name that the street was the one I'd

seen early that morning. Then I saw a bridge, very near and shaped like the Golden Gate Bridge, except for its silver-gray color—and that disoriented my sense of place and direction. I thought the dull orange top of the bridge I'd seen in the park was none other than the Golden Gate Bridge itself, yet the bridge I now saw looked just like it.

Lilian turned around the corner of the parking lot. I noticed an employment agency across K-Li Jear, Clay Street. My view became bright—the sky began to clear. I committed the geography of the area to memory.

We went to a restaurant on Kearny Street. I felt awkward, compelled to dine at the same table with my father and a stranger, two grown-ups twice my age, receiving alms from them.

I peered at my father, wondering how he could eat, not with the inhibition befitting a guest, but with such ease and the all-out enjoyment befitting an old friend. He gathered the dishes to the center of the table, adjusted the position of the bowls and teacups so they wouldn't stand in the way of Lilian's elbows.

Lilian too pushed the dishes toward my father and me, a gesture to prompt us to eat freely. She had seen how I tried not to make sounds when chewing and ladling and sipping the soup, not to hit my spoon against the bowl. She tried not to catch my sullen eyes so I could be more at ease, not knowing that I was observing how my father behaved like a host.

He clucked his tongue when he was done, let out ums and uhs of satisfaction as he sipped the tea. Odder still, when it came time to pay, he did not protest, did not snatch the bill over as he used to do back in Laos, fighting with his friends to pay it.

Lilian slipped a ten-dollar bill under the upturned check. I shot a glance at my father, who was blindly munching a fortune cookie. The swamp of my anger churned in a turmoil. I glared.

On the street, Lilian suggested going to the movies.

Movies? Watching movies has no use for the mind or the body. A big waste of time, my father objected.

I frowned, surprised that Lilian could not only get along but go along with my father, who could be so arrogant. Why did she humor him?

Better walk around. Get exercise that way, my father said, passing the movie theater without stopping.

I sulked, following along. We walked around some more. Elbow to elbow, we could hardly turn. The fish stores, grocers, teahouses, restaurants, bakeries, herbalist shops, photo shops, hair salons, bookstores, hotels.

My mother would have liked to shop here, elbow to elbow, heel to heel. She would have liked to buy a pound of shrimp or a soy-sauce chicken.

Ahma, in the refugee camp, had told me, Remember to go to the temple and have a monk read the sutra for your mom and sister. If Ahma can move, Ahma will cook something for them, and bring it to the temple. Shrimp is your mom's favorite. She told me in a dream she craves shrimp.

I pictured my mother and sister hungry, their family neglecting to feed them. Their souls wandered along the Mekong, along the border, while my father and I dined out with a woman in San Francisco Chinatown. I happened to look up: a mass of fast-flying clouds coming over the sun.

Lilian, my father, and I could hardly turn, elbow to elbow, heel to heel. The crowd frustrated my father. We left Chinatown and, after driving around some more, ended up at the Cow Palace.

It was Lilian's idea, to see the circus. I could care less. All I knew about circuses I'd learned from a children's magazine my parents subscribed to, my favorite. The *Children's Playground* was published in Hong Kong (the notorious opium den according to action films), then airshipped to Bangkok (an even more notorious capital of drug traffic), then airshipped again from Bangkok to Vientiane (the capital of the Kingdom of a Million Elephants, more figurative than factual); then transported from Vientiane to Luang Prabang, where the magazines were unloaded and later distributed to drug the eager schoolchildren like me who broke into a thousand smiles at the sound and sight of the lone motorcyclist who delivered the magazines to my home.

Again my father surprised me by gladly going along and letting her pay for the tickets.

The Palace began to fill. A family came over and took the seats in front of us. Lilian found her view blocked by a large man. She leaned right, left, stretched her neck—to no avail. All she saw was his large head and large shoulders. She didn't ask my father to trade seats. She reached over, tapped the back of the seat, in case the large man couldn't hear her or understand her English. Askyouseeme, askyouseeme, I cannot see. The giant turned around. She with a smile waved her hand back and forth, to signal that he blocked her view.

Oh, I'm sorry, the gentle giant roared, and stood up. He exchanged the seat with his child sitting next to him, and sat down in front of me. Would I tap the giant's back? Should we sit somewhere else? Again Lilian reached over.

We ended up switching seats: the three refugees moved to the front row; the giant and his not-so-giant family, a family of three, moved to the back.

Sometime during the show the terrorist of fear crashed through the wall of the Palace and, backflipping, again machinegunned the audience. Lilian let out a gasp and covered her mouth with a hand, as she watched a man prepared to throw a flying knife at a spinning target where a woman in a swimsuit was pinioned in the middle.

The drumming quickened, to simulate the heartbeat of the Palace, as the man prepared to throw. The cloaked magician threw the flying knife. The Palace gasped. Just then a smoke screen burst and a tiger leaped out from the thick of it onto the stage and right behind it jumped out the woman in the swimsuit. Triumphant and free, and with a big smile, she waved to the audience.

The Palace roared. Lilian clapped and smiled happily. I clapped along with everyone else. Just then the tiger snarled, baring its white fangs, prepared to claw at, to pounce on, the innocently smiling lady in front of it and to outroar the Palace in the vehemence of its attack.

The lady happened to turn around—in time to see the paw hovering over her fragile skull. Terror struck her at the inevitability of her being crushed to pulp. The Palace hushed.

Under the intensity of the audience's attention, the fragile lady began—brave soul—to speak. She ordered the tiger to step down from its height. The tiger stepped down, but that was not all: he knelt down obediently under the command of her fragile voice. The audience roared again, overcome with the human docility of the beast.

I enjoyed the circus. Laughter had left me weak by the time the elephant troupe came on stage to dance, and, clumsily, kept missing steps. Laughing so hard, I didn't notice if my father laughed along, if he enjoyed the circus too, or simply sat there like a rock, suffering the big waste of his time. Lilian herself laughed till her chair shook.

After the circus Lilian took us to a pizza parlor. And again she took out her purse. Munching slowly, she watched us eat our first pizza ever. In our jackets with alternate light and dark blue stripes, we sat holding our pizza and chewing the crispy crust and the cheesy layer on its top. We chewed energetically, swallowed, took another big bite.

I would remember my first slice as the best I ever had, because none of the pizza I had in subsequent years ever equaled it, not even the pizza from that same pizza parlor.

WRONG SON

I was sitting in the kitchen when the doorbell rang. Lilian went to open the door. Exclamations and greetings—a man's, a woman's, and children's—burst from the door to the living room and the kitchen. Where was my father? I hoped the guests had not seen me. I dreaded thinking about how the hostess would introduce me.

Would she tell her guests that I was merely a visitor? Or a new housemate? A desperate relative? The future stepson? A refugee!

From Vietnam—the nosy guests would assume, because they had seen boat people on TV. The guests would gossip about me. The harrowing experience of escape, they would say, had made him so scrawny and jaundiced.

I was trapped in the kitchen.

Lilian was receiving her guests in the living room when the doorbell rang again. Another burst of greetings and exclamations. A baby cried. Voices began to jumble. A man, the crying baby's father, entered the kitchen looking for a cup while Lilian called out where to look for it. He found the cupboard, fetched a cup, and left, without seeing me.

Lilian came in. Why don't you come to the living room and sit down with us?

I'm fine here. I didn't know what to do with my hands—whether to cross them or put them squarely on the table.

She smiled, and left me alone.

I returned to the bedroom, the cube with its windows and shutters closed. I felt uncaged and free. I jumped into the bed, pulled the blanket that Lilian had lent me, with its foreign smell, up to my chin, but I couldn't shut out the noise.

A mother admonished her naughty son. Don't. Stop that. Don't jump on the sofa.

A sharp slap, and the burst of a cry, defiant and strident. As it diminished to a tired sob later, a father spoke. Annie, oh look, look at Annie. Don't chew the flowers. Silly girl, you can't eat them. See this? The father must have been showing a flower to the tearful girl. It's plastic. Getting hungry, huh? Huh? My silly girl. Time for milk.

The girl started to cry.

The refugee-housemate-guest looked at the alarm clock. Past four-thirty.

Another mother's shriek. Frankie, I told you to stop jumping on the sofa. You deaf? Auntie Lilian'll kill you.

I slipped from the bedroom into the hallway. In the living room a boy was still jumping on the sofa, treating it as a springboard. Three girls clustered around the lamp table with a fake jade vase in the middle, playing with the plastic flowers. The sound of mah-jongg from the kitchen. I tiptoed to the front door, opened it, went downstairs.

Once I was on the street, the cool light breeze swept me and the sun felt warm. I closed my eyes, turned my face toward the sun, and took a deep breath. I walked down Fulton Street alongside Golden Gate Park, toward the ocean twenty blocks away. The horizon shone silver in the sun.

As I walked, I smelled kafir lime, a strong smell. I sniffed, looked around me to trace the scent, but saw only the eucalyptus trees on the slope, not the kafir-lime tree at all. A sea-gull soared by leisurely. I walked up the slope to look some more and saw ahead a small forest of thick big trees; no kafir lime. Yet the unmistakable scent. I inhaled.

When I came back, I still didn't see my father. The walk down Fulton Street and up, a total of forty blocks, exhausted me. I opened the door as lightly and slowly as possible, enough to slip through. With the hubbub of the children in the living room, no one noticed me.

In the privacy of the bedroom, in bed, I heard the spatula scraping against the wok and sizzling—my nerves too siz-zled—as Lilian added water or vegetables to the heated wok. My stomach growled. Lilian talked and laughed with her guests while cooking. I turned over, toward the wall.

At last dinner must have been ready. I heard my father talk-ing to Lilian. A few moments later, my eyes shut, I heard the door open. My father called me. I kept my eyes shut. He closed the door ten seconds later. I blinked. Then I heard the *clink-clank* of the tableware and Lilian asking about me. My father replied, He's sleeping. Let him sleep.

My father talked to the guests. I tried to fall asleep. By eight-thirty the dinner was still going on. Why wouldn't they finish soon and leave? So I could get something to eat in the kitchen. Eventually I fell asleep. When I got up—what time was it?—I felt grouchy, my stomach empty.

During the following weekends Lilian hosted dinner par-ties.

One group of guests—her colleagues at the bank—spoke Cantonese. Lilian liked to play the records of Sam Hui, a Hong Kong pop singer, for them, though she ended up turning off the stereo because their noisy children made it impossible to hear the music.

The next group would speak Mandarin. They might have come from Indochina because their Mandarin had the accent familiar to me. They appeared so at home in San Francisco, I couldn't tell they were refugees. How had Lilian come to be-friend them? Were they her distant relatives? None spoke Laotian to her.

Although she did not cook Laotian food to entertain her guests, Lilian turned out a variety of Chinese dishes. Always something new and tasty on the few occasions I felt compelled to join her dinner parties—when I didn't pretend to be sleeping or go for a walk, down the twenty blocks or so to the ocean.

I would sit gingerly among the guests with my father, but when I ate, I relished the food and inwardly praised Lilian's cooking. The tender beef in the rich sauce that she concocted was such a satisfaction to the tongue. The guests cracked one joke after another, making every one at the table burst into hearty laughter. I laughed too. They did not interrogate me. They probably thought I was a guest.

My father and I had been in San Francisco for a few weeks, during which time he called Karen once. Neither of us had contacted Uncle Chao.

I waited to see what my father would do next, for of course we could not stay on with Lilian.

Time to move on, into a place of our own. I waited for my father to make the move. Yet he had said nothing about mov-ing out or moving on: it seemed that he had decided to settle down in Lilian's apartment.

Rather than wait, I acted. One morning I told my father I was going to Chinatown.

Good, he said. Go outside. Stretch your body. Get some fresh air. See the world. It does you good. Did I need coins for the bus? I said no. He shoved them into my palm anyway.

I walked down Geary Boulevard with a map in my pocket and took bus 38. According to the route I'd mapped out, I would get off at a street named Powell and turn left, walk all the way, then turn right at Clay. Straightforward. Impossible to get lost.

After I got off, I followed the map. I crossed the street. The cable car jingled and rumbled along the track. I made way for pedestrians, holding on to the map in case a pickpocket stole it.

The street led me uphill. I kept on. It led me steadily up. The wind blew against my hair and my eyes, flattening the legs of my jeans. At an intersection I turned around for a view of the high-rises and the traffic below: cars, buses, and pedestrians reduced in size. When I found Clay Street I turned right.

I headed steadily downhill and began to see store signs in Chinese. More signs vertical and horizontal, with large picture words. Chinatown! And soon, scuttling down Clay, I spotted the underground lot where Lilian had parked. Before long I saw the employment agency on my side of the street.

Taking a deep breath, I knocked at the glass door. A man sat behind a desk. After I stepped in, I told him what I had come for; I'd decided to act American, so I dropped the polite "you" in Mandarin when I addressed him.

One job was in Japantown. Good location—right on Geary, where I could catch the bus. Seven hundred and fifty dollars a month. Ten hours a day. Not eight hours? No. From eleven a.m. to nine p.m. That would mean no time for school, no time for study. But why not get a job first? I could then hire a tutor. But ten hours of washing dishes every day? I'd never done this. I could quit after a month if I couldn't take it. First I needed to make the sacrifice. Just think, $750 a month.

The man made a phone call to set up the interview in Japantown. He scribbled a note and gave it to me—the address and the phone number. He wouldn't charge the agency fee until I started work, he said.

To facilitate digestion after dinner, I took a walk with my father down Fulton toward the ocean. Past six, yet it was still daylight.

I told my father about the job and my decision to work. I felt good, the words emptied out from my chest. Seven hundred and fifty dollars a month, I added.

He merely said, You'll need a pair of gloves to wash dishes, and the water should be warm.

I just want to try it, to see what it is like. I felt the need to emphasize that the job was for a short term only, to reassure him.

We crossed the parking lot and arrived at the beach in time to see a beautiful sunset. Orange clouds hung far up in the sky. We went to the seawall. The tide was low. The wind messed up our hair. We walked on, and as we crossed the parking lot we saw bus 38 arriving at a stop.

Look—he chuckled—bus 38, it comes all the way here, finding this simple fact a joy.

From now on I could hop onto the bus to go to the beach, whenever I liked.

The sky turned deep blue. We walked up Balboa and went to Geary Boulevard, where the traffic bustled. A clear night, no fog, no clouds, the promise of a sunny tomorrow. We passed a produce store, discovered a Thai restaurant, stopped by a movie house to see what was playing, before heading back to the apartment, ready for sleep.

The sunny blue sky on next day made me confident about my first job interview. Surely, I would get the job. The bus took me to Japantown.

I found the restaurant easily. The number on the door matched the note in my hand. I peered into the glass door—the outdoor blue sky made the indoor appear dark and cool. Inside, chairs were placed upside down on the tables, a woman mopping the floor. She moved slowly, bending her back, oblivious of my knocks on the door.

I stopped knocking, my knuckles beginning to hurt. I decided to use my fist and pounded. Only then did she turn, as if awakening from a stupor. I pointed at the doorknob inside and gestured to her. She turned away, continued to mop. I pounded again. She dropped the mop, went to the door, pointed at the "closed" sign.

I shook my head, to show her I was not a customer, and pointed at the note in my hand, shoved it forward to the glass wall to better show it, until she took one more slow step forward to the door and opened it.

What? She squinted.

I come here to see a Mr. Chan.

Not open yet!

I don't come here to eat. I handed her the note. Is there a Mr. Chan here? Mr. Chan?

She ignored the note and pointed at the "closed" sign. Closed, she yelled impatiently.

I'm here to see Mr. Chan.

I told you there's nobody here.

This is the Big-One Restaurant?

She scowled at me. Where do your eyes grow? Can't you see?

I blushed. I need to see Mr. Chan. I'm told he'll be in after nine.

She stared at me. Then she turned away and headed inside, leaving the door ajar. Follow me. She kept walking.

I slipped in, closed the door, and followed her, careful not to step on the wet floor where she had just mopped. At the kitchen door I stopped. Old men and women wearing dirty white aprons were cutting vegetables and cleaning the sink and putting bowls away, a man kneading flour dough, a woman carrying a bucket of water.

The woman walked toward the old man kneading the dough. She said something to him. He turned. Meanwhile the woman headed for the kitchen door, passed me, and went to pick up the mop.

The old man told me to come over.

You're Mr. Chan? I stepped up.

He didn't answer, but said, Tell me what you want, and kept on with his work.

I had no choice but to forgo formality and tell him.

Don't you go to school? Not looking at me, kneading the dough.

I said no, and added that I'd just come to California.

From where?

I told him, unsure if he understood.

Oh, so you come from the war zone, he said.

The war zone? I made no answer.

He raised his eyebrows and repeated the question.

No answer.

Yes? He raised his voice, pressing for a response.

I kept silent. It was not the way I referred to my homeland: the site of ravage.

Why don't you go to school? As loud as ever. Others must have heard. I told the man why, just as loud. Let them hear.

My son, he finally faced me, you too young for work. You should use your heart for school first. Go use your heart for school. As if work were truancy, a prank.

I'll go to school later but now I need a job—

Can you work like we do? Cutting vegetables, washing dishes, ten hours a day. Seven days a week. No rest. If you break a dish, you pay for it. If you break five, you get fired. Can you work like us?

I nodded, though doubt had set in.

He ignored my nod. You too young. We can't hire you. Go to school first.

I blurted out, I thought this is a free country. If I want to work, I can work. I don't have to be too old or too young to work, right?

Wrong, son. The law says you're not old enough to work—

I rushed out of the kitchen, headed straight for the front door, stepped right over the area where the woman had just mopped, without looking back, yanked the door open, darted out. Breathing heavily, I paced back and forth at the bus stop. When the bus arrived I bolted in.

After dinner I overheard my father tell Lilian in the kitchen,

Wants to wash dishes. Let him learn his lesson. Else he won't know, following this with a chuckle.

My father telling my private business to someone else? I unlocked the door, bolted down the stairs, half ran half walked on the street, down the few blocks to Golden Gate Park. The fog passed through the top branches of the eucalyptus and the cypresses.

Sunshine was short-lived that day. Around noon, shortly after my job interview, the fog began to roll in, and by twelve-thirty not a patch of blue remained in the sky above the Richmond district.

I circled the pond, catching my breath, and still panting hard, I noticed that a large black car moved along the pond with me. I turned away, kept walking quickly.

When I turned around again, I saw that the black window had rolled down, a bald and puffy-faced man smiling in the coffin-looking car. I kept walking. The limousine drove after me faster and closer. I turned around and saw the window already rolled back up, the car a polished black object.

I had read in the Chinese newspaper about a woman whose body was found cut up in a garbage can by the beach, and seen messages on milk cartons with photos of missing youngsters. And Lilian's warning about the black-glove society. I pictured the man snickering and watching me behind the rolled-up window.

I left the pond and ran up the trail. The car sped up but stopped at the entrance of the trail. My feet began to shake. I didn't dare to look back or stop to catch my breath. When I took a quick glance back, I saw no car. I kept running. The trees swept past me when again I saw the black top of the car moving on the driveway to the left of the trail, keeping pace with me, the man smiling.

I tore down the trail on the opposite side of the slope. I tore through the bushes and shot across Fulton Street without turning to check the traffic. I ran up a street sucking air through my mouth but decided to turn around the corner in case the coffin car came from behind. At the end of the block I turned another corner, and another.

Then I found myself on the street where Lilian lived. I darted into the apartment, darted into the bedroom, panted even harder. I couldn't sit, couldn't stand.

A moment later I picked up the phone to call Uncle Chao.

SUPERMAN

Brother, Uncle Chao told my father, with your talent, you'll make big money in America. You know how to fix houses—this skill alone will make you rich.

I had just entered the first grade. My family gathered around the table. As the adults talked, I flipped through the stack of photographs Uncle had brought. Glimpses of the Golden Gate Bridge passed my eyes.

My mother enjoyed Uncle's stories of America, but said, Our family is here. Why leave home for a strange land?

To dig gold, Uncle replied. You know Laos is a poor country, Sister. You don't even have a refrigerator or a phone.

We have a good life. Any further mention of the fighting between the royal troops and the Pathet Lao, the cannons and machine guns we heard at night, from the outskirts, would sound repetitious: the war in Indochina had gone on too long—even before my birth, even before my mother sent my uncle abroad.

They need carpenters in America. You'll make lots of money, Brother, Uncle said.

Your brother-in-law has a wood shop to oversee, my mother reminded her younger brother.

No matter. They need carpenters in America. If you go there you'll get rich. I guarantee it.

I leaned over the sofa by the window to part the curtains, and peered down at the driveway below. A sedan pulled up and parked in the driveway. I leaned away from the parted curtain and sat back down on the sofa. A few moments later the doorbell rang. I ran to the door to open it, and sure enough, Uncle Chao, who looked the same after almost ten years, stood outside the door.

A well-dressed woman, a head shorter than Uncle Chao and carrying a shiny black purse, followed him into Lilian's apartment. You must be— Upon seeing me, she exclaimed in a heavy accent as if she had more trouble speaking English than I did. Before I heard the rest, she already clamped me tightly in her arms. I began to wriggle my shoulders to disengage myself, but she had pulled me to her, her purse pressed on my back. I felt I should do something with my hands, but before I could do anything, she freed me from her arms. Her eyes had become red and moist.

Now, now, don't start. You'll make him cry, Uncle Chao cautioned his wife.

She wiped her eyes with a handkerchief and broke into a smile at the same time, her large earrings swinging.

Don't mention it to him. Remember, Uncle whispered to her in Vietnamese.

In fact I knew enough Vietnamese to understand them. He might as well have mentioned my mother to me directly.

My father came to the door to greet Uncle Chao. Neither had seen the other for close to a decade. But as they made their greetings, neither mentioned my mother. Uncle introduced his wife to my father in Cantonese. She's half-Chinese, half-Vietnamese, came from Laos.

So Sister speaks all these languages, my father remarked.

She nodded.

You've grown, Uncle Chao said to me, and turned to his wife, When I saw him last, he was only this tall, estimating my height with his hand. The boy had a crew cut then, the soldier's cut. Just this bit tall.

Uncle still looks the same, I said.

Auntie Chao chuckled. We've been waiting for your call. We know you're coming but we don't know the date. We waited and wondered what happened.

I cast my father a glance.

When Auntie Chao asked whom we stayed with, my father said it was a friend, who had left for work.

I sometimes work on Saturday too, Auntie said.

The pace of life is fast here, Uncle Chao said. People always in a rush. Time is money.

Time is money only when you count it in dollars. She pronounced "dollar" as dough-la.

Having been introduced to my uncle and aunt's all-time favorite subject of conversation, my father nodded. Do you still run the restaurant business?

Uncle Chao shook his hand. No more. Everyone who can't speak English wants to open a restaurant here. Old Gold Mountain already has too many. Hard to compete, hard to make a profit.

Then what do you do now?

Business. He wouldn't specify. I later learned that he guarded all details about his work, keeping his privacy the American way.

What do you do, Sis?

I have a beauty shop. Cosmetics business. Nothing beats working for oneself. What about you, Brother?

I'm a carpenter.

It has never been easy for carpenters to get jobs, Uncle Chao said, reversing his opinion of a decade ago. Such hard work. How do you compete with Americans larger and faster than you?

Just do what one can, the best one can. My father sighed.

Uncle Chao told him, Don't count on getting rich here. Put the thought away the sooner the better, especially when you can't speak English. Don't let the abundance of Gold Mountain oranges here mislead your eyes and start you thinking that gold is as plenty. You can work all your life but it won't make you rich. You can only scrape by.

I stared at Uncle and wondered why my father said nothing—he would be a fool if he let Uncle Chao's words get to him and lived by them. But I was too naive, too new to America, to make Uncle Chao retract his nonsense, but my father's later behavior displayed signs whose source I could trace to this moment. I stared at Uncle Chao.

A fortune takes time to build. Saving is also important, Auntie said. We want to take you out for lunch, Brother. And— She turned to me. Ah-Ming, come over and stay with uncle and your cousins.

It was only within the family that my name was used. It sounded so foreign, under the circumstances.

Right, that's the idea, my father said. Go and stay with your cousins and get to know them.

Has he ever met them? Uncle Chao asked.

I don't think so. Auntie said, and looked to me. But you'll meet them soon. They're on a camping trip this weekend. You can go to school with your cousins.

And learn English from them, Uncle Chao said.

Wonderful, right on right on. My father nodded vigorously.

Do they speak Chinese and Lao? I opened my mouth.

Very little. Mostly they speak English. Her eyes lighted up, she beamed with the pride of a parent whose children spoke fluent, faultless English. How much English do you know?

Some.

He said he knows some English, she told her husband in English, who surely must have heard me.

They prompted me to get ready. Bring what you need for now, my father said. I will bring the rest over in a week; just pack what you can.

He followed me into the bedroom.

Aren't you going to pack too? I asked.

He stayed still.

Aren't you coming along? I asked again.

I will only stay overnight, he said. I have to return to San Francisco, making it sound like he went out of his way for my sake, making me feel I was standing in his way.

I stared at him.

Go, go. He waved me away. Go stay with your cousins. Learn English from them.

Biting my lower lip, I bent down to pack. He always shoved me over to other families. I had no sense of home anymore.

As I packed, he continued, You can go to school with your cousins. Use the opportunity. Else you'll miss school. My situation is un—

I don't want to hear it, I shouted. I grabbed the bag and rushed to the hallway without looking at him.

He followed me to the hallway.

I ran downstairs and shot out of the apartment. On the street, I realized that Uncle and Auntie were still in Lilian's apartment. I dropped the bag by Uncle's car door and returned upstairs.

I kept to myself during the ride. I wouldn't look at my father seated beside me in the back. Why would he want to stay with Lilian? No doubt he sweet-talked his way into staying with her rent-free.

Driving, Uncle Chao told his wife again what I'd said about him: He said I look the same.

She laughed and turned around. So you think your uncle still looks young, huh, Ming?

I forced a smile.

He last saw me about ten years ago, during my visit to Laos, Uncle told Auntie.

Ten years ago his hair was straight and black. Now he had a perm and only half of his hair looked black. And the less one said about his perm or his attempt at being modern American, the better.

Still as young as ever, she teased her husband, her eyes sparkling with a smile. Is it true? she asked him, and while chuckling, reached over the seat to pat his face.

Uncle Chao smiled, probably thinking: What would a kid know? Still wet behind the ears. He addressed me. Speak English now, huh, in his heavy accent as if he had just learned to speak English himself. You're in America now. You need to speak English. But then he slipped into Cantonese. No more Lao. No Thai. That you can forget. Speak of San Francisco as San Francisco, not Sarm Farn Si or Sam Fun Shee either, or Sand Fan as the Lao would say. Sounds so ugly, Sand Fan. Say San Fran Cis Co. Say it.

Auntie Chao chuckled. He'll learn in time. Right, Ming?

Uncle Chao continued to advise me in Cantonese. You've got to train yourself to think in English from now on. Then to his wife in English: Why don't we give him an American name?

She smiled. Your uncle's American name is Tony, she told me in English. You can call him Uncle Tony.

I had been gazing at my uncle's perm—I couldn't help but do so, because his modern hairstyle loomed in front of me and had preempted everything else in my vision ever since he'd gotten in the driver's seat—and now, upon learning my uncle's stylish name, I peered sideways at my father. My father showed no other reaction but an all-accommodating smile, looking as innocent as his black hair must have appeared to his in-laws.

Now, what will it be? Uncle Chao muttered in Cantonese.

How about George?

Joe? Uncle Chao echoed. His "George" sounded like "Joe."

Or Stanley. George or Stanley. They both sound nice. How do you like George? She turned to me. I think Stanley fits you better.

Joe sounds good, Uncle Chao said.

I don't need an English name, I spoke up. My name is fine as it is.

Auntie Chao turned. Why don't you want one? You can make American friends.

I like my name the way it is, I repeated. I'm not a Westerner. I don't need a Western name.

This guy's too Asian, Uncle Chao said to his wife in English.

People won't remember your Chinese or Lao name, Auntie told me.

They won't know you and you won't make any friends, Uncle Chao said.

Now, what's your Lao name?

Boontakorn.

What? What is it? Uncle Chao asked loudly, exaggeratedly, pricking up his ear. Say that again.

Boontakorn.

See? It's a difficult name to learn, Auntie noted. Don't you want to make American friends?

If they don't want to take the time to know my name, fine, I don't care to make friends with them either.

Uncle Chao didn't choose to comment, but turned away to look out the window, his mouth puckered up slightly. He looked smug.

There's no rush. You can think about it. I still think Stanley fits you. Auntie Chao smiled. A forced smile.

I felt uneasy and regretted that I had blurted out.

My father remarked, He has a stubborn streak about him. Hard-neck.

*　　*　　*

Auntie Chao showed me my cousin's room that I was to share: a tennis racket hung on the wall, a violin in a corner, trophies of various sorts and a photo of my cousin on the desk, a pair of boxing gloves on the bed. This cousin of mine must be quite talented, in addition to being a fluent speaker of English. I let out a quick but short string of compliments. My aunt beamed. What parent could resist hearing her children being complimented? Least of all my aunt. I remembered how she smiled and her eyes lighted up when she had talked about her children earlier. Her immense pleasure reinforced the notion that parents' favorite subject of conversation must have been their children. My father joined in the compliment of my cousin's talent, what a strapping young man, how athletic, an ideal role model for me, much to the recipient's content.

My father spent the night in my cousin's room, among the trophies. The next morning Uncle Chao drove him back to San Francisco.

Later, around noon, in the kitchen, Uncle Chao filled the rice cooker with about two cups of rice from a container. He then opened the tap, washed the rice. I had never seen him in the kitchen doing chores. It seemed improper for me, as the junior one, to just watch him. I offered help. But he declined instantly because he, as the uncle, had seniority. Auntie, in a lavender sweatsuit, came to the kitchen to help.

She still had her makeup and earrings on. Her hands well manicured—long red nails. She had the blessed look: her somewhat overweight body signaled blessing and luck. Which made up for her lanky husband's supposed lack of it, lankiness portending a life of hardship. So, their large home, with a tall-ceilinged living room, a spacious kitchen, a large clean bathroom, and four cars, served as the testament of their hardship, their untoward destiny.

At the dining table Uncle Chao, as he saw me slouch, told me to sit with my back straight. Put some spirit into the spine.

Feet on the floor. No droopy shoulders. Don't act like an opium eater. So I straightened my back against the chair. My feet dangled off it.

Uncle Chao prompted me, Eat, eat, motioning with his chopsticks. We had a plate of "plainly chopped chicken" and roast duck.

Eat and grow like a big boy, my aunt said.

This is not like Laos. Here you can eat as much as you want. I nodded.

She said, You are in America, not Laos—as if I didn't know it—so don't worry about eating up the food.

Uncle Chao told her, with the air of a reporter, Back there, people have only a pinch of meat with a bowl of rice, a small plate of salted fish for the whole family. As if he were the only person privy to this stale fact.

Auntie chuckled, eyeing me with her bright eyes. I laughed too. The way my uncle said it—his English—made the reality of having only salted fish with rice for a meal appear comical.

Auntie said, Look what we have here. So many choices. So eat. Don't worry about tomorrow.

Uncle Chao held a drumstick with his chopsticks over to me. I received it with my bowl and went on stirring the rice with the chopsticks.

He said, In America people say thank you when someone gives you something.

I looked up.

No matter how small the thing is, when someone gives you something, no matter what it is, you say thank you.

I nodded and started to eat when I heard him: Say it, then. Say it out.

Could it be that Uncle was waiting for me to say thank you? I looked at my aunt. She merely smiled. I said, I feel awkward about saying thank you to one's own relatives. We don't say it out.

They exchanged a look. My aunt laughed.

But this is America. Leave the Lao part behind. And forget the Chinese side of you. It doesn't get you anywhere, Uncle Chao said.

You mean even when you give me a drumstick, I still have to say thank you?

Yes, you say thank you.

To you?

Yes.

Do I say it now?

Yes. They looked incredulous.

I said, Tank you. I hadn't yet mastered the "the" sound.

Auntie Chao said, No one's going to understand you if you just nod.

What's so hard about saying thank you?

Aren't we supposed to keep thank you inside? I was taught to keep it inside and feel thankful. I don't say it out.

Useless, said Uncle Chao. It's too uptight, the Chinese weakling way. Then, in English, Do you know "uptight"?

Uptight?

Nodding is passive, Auntie said.

After lunch Uncle Chao asked me to take down the papaya from the altar in the living room.

I saw in the altar a framed photograph, black-and-white, of my grandfather. In his eyes I saw my mother. The gaze. The smile. In front of the picture stood a small cup of un-cooked rice, with a few sticks of incense inserted in the middle. By the side of the incense lay a ripe papaya, in a saucer. Why are you standing there? Mother asked. Come closer. Bow to Ah-Goong. Remember Ah-Goong? I pulled a chair to the front of the altar and stepped up onto the chair to bow. Grandfather eyed me dotingly. You've grown tall. Let Ah-Goong take a good look at you. Grandfather reached over. Step closer so Ah-Goong can see you better, Mother prompted me.

When I returned with the papaya, I found Uncle speaking

to Auntie in Vietnamese. They were talking about me. Fine, fine, I'll ask, she said as she washed the dishes.

I sat down at the table, not letting out that I understood what they said. They had assumed I didn't know Vietnamese. Uncle Chao began to peel the papaya.

Facing the sink, with the sound of water squirting from the faucet, Auntie asked me in English if I liked to live in San Francisco or Milpitas.

In San Francisco? I thought of Lilian's dinner parties. In Milpitas with Uncle? I had no ready answer.

Auntie said, Give the matter some thought. Milpitas has good schools. But now we want to take you to buy shoes.

I felt thankful for their gesture of kindness and realized I should say thank you, but the thought—a second of hesitation—made it even harder to say. When another second passed, my tongue had grown stiff. Finally I gave up, because ten seconds later my thank-you would sound as out of place as thanking him when earlier he'd said, This guy's too Asian.

Uncle Chao said my sneakers, the pair I bought in downtown Nongkhai, outside the refugee camp, looked too shabby. Time to throw them away, he said.

I gave him a wondering look, insulted. I said they still fit.

Wouldn't you rather have new shoes? He sounded impatient.

No. I like mine. I find them comfortable, I said. The real reason was that they, though dirty and worn, had crossed countries, the Pacific, and the continents with me. I couldn't part with them.

Uncle Chao turned around and told his wife in Vietnamese, this guy is too picky. He kept "picky" in English.

Do you know "picky"? She asked me in English.

I shook my head. What is "piggy"?

Picky is choosy. Do you know "choosy"?

On the way to buy shoes, Uncle Chao, driving, asked me if I had heard "Saturday Night Fever." I looked at him blankly. He asked again, Do you know disco?

An easy word to say and remember. I shook my head.

Let him listen to some Bee Gee, Uncle told his wife.

Auntie Chao bent a little forward to reach for the radio. She tried out different stations before settling for one.

Is dis disgo? I pushed the question.

From the radio: *Young men . . . I say young men.*

Yes, dis is disgo. She smiled. *Y-M-C-A. Y-M-C-A.* Good music?

The Village People, Uncle Chao said. Number one. He raised his left thumb.

Just then we got into a traffic jam. Cars stopped moving. A few people began to honk. Police cars with sirens on tried to get through. I looked outside the window. I recognized the pyramid landmark. We had gotten off the freeway. Just then, on the street, a flying human raced like a bullet over the grayish counterpart of the Golden Gate Bridge.

I recognized the flying human immediately. There was no mistaking it. Superman! I called out, and rolled down the window. Superman! My hand reached outside the window, waving frantically.

People stuck in the traffic jam hailed and cheered; some clapped.

Then I saw, in a distance, the commotion on the bridge: a bus dangled on the verge of the bridge, about to plunge into the bay.

As always, Superman arrived at the scene in time. With arms stretched out in front, he flew into the stranded bus, slowed down while he made a turn and gauged the situation. He came to the side of the bus and—amid the panic of the passengers, which was transformed into bright optimism as soon as they saw him in midair outside the bus—descended vertically until he reached under the endangered vehicle; he then lifted it up with one arm, and when it was level with the railing, he held it with both hands and put it gently, with seeming ease, back inside the safety of the bridge. The passengers swarmed to the windows, only to see their favorite savior waving good-bye as he hurried off with lightning speed, ready to respond to another crisis, leaving the local police to take care of the rest of the scene of the accident.

Uncle Chao heaved a sigh of relief. We all did, thankful that we had Superman around, ready for any emergency. We waved at the figure flying away even though he was far above the high-rises with rows and columns of windows and couldn't have seen us. Other people too waved from their cars and cheered. After the excitement had subsided a notch, Uncle Chao started the car.

I knew I would see Superman, live.

BUTTERFLIES ON THE BLANKET

I started school the day after Uncle Chao took care of the registration. I put on the same pair of shoes. That day we left the shoe shop empty-handed—because I couldn't find any shoes that would fit me, though Uncle was convinced that I was "picky." I put on the same pair of jeans I had worn for a few days. I'd wanted to ask my aunt where I could wash the jeans but she seemed to be in a sour mood. The corner of her mouth puckered up. The two clumps of dark clouds that were her eyebrows packed in a permanent frown. What was irritating her? By scolding her children at seven in the morning, she gave vent to her mood. No breakfast on the table.

I left for school with my well-groomed cousin Michael, with whom I shared a bedroom. It turned out that school served breakfast. In the cafeteria, Michael's classmates, upon introduction, looked at me and probably wondered why I stared blankly at them instead of speaking. They looked as if they were ready for a fight, sitting at the table, their voices so loud, their bodies taking up a lot of space.

A black student arrived at the table with a breakfast tray.

Michael again made the introduction before she sat down. Within one minute of our acquaintance, she told me she had a feeling we would become good friends. The newspapers were right: Americans love to exaggerate! But I was trained to regard friendship as something that took years to cultivate—and then to be further tested. So I didn't quite know what to say to the girl.

Should I say something as a gesture of friendliness? But what?

Michael and the other students at the table talked loudly and fast, not at all interested in eating. They poked at their breakfast, gulped down milk as if it were water, and continued their vivacious conversation, noisier than sparrows. I caught the eyes of the black girl. Her eyes seemed to speak: Say something, you, let's be friends.

I could tell her about the Laotian girl who went to New York by herself. We had to transfer at the Seattle airport, the group of us who'd left the camp in the same bus and gone to Bangkok to take the jet to North America. In Bangkok, the Thai officials put all of us in a building. They figured since we all wanted to go to America badly, we would not run away. They figured we would behave. For the first time they allowed us to go to places without a pass. We stayed in Bangkok for about ten days. We took the jumbo jet to Hong Kong, then to Tokyo, then Seattle. At the Seattle airport our group parted, each family to head for a different destination. No one but the girl was going to New York. She wore a sarong, a pair of slippers, with socks. She pleaded with one of the families to go with her and not to leave her. She clung to a woman's hands, crying in public. She became frantic as we started looking for the terminals. The girl pulled at the woman's hands and begged the woman not to leave her there. I did not see the girl again.

But how would I tell this to the girl at my table? She was talking to the boys, their expressions animated.

The bell rang.

All eyes zoomed in on me as I followed Michael into the noisy classroom. Students left their seats and horsed around while the teacher, the man at the podium, looked at something with a pen in his hand. He did not see that a new student had walked in.

I felt odd, like a curiosity being sized up, as Michael led me to the podium. The teacher simply told me to sit down first. He raised his hands and voice and told the whole class to sit down. I sat next to my cousin. The teacher still did not seem to note that he had a new student.

I learned two words during the first period: "scoff" and "meticulous." When the teacher read out the vocabulary, the words seemed to ride on a rapid of syllables. Some students left their desks to scramble for a dictionary on the shelf.

Michael leaned back in the seat. Didn't he need a dictionary? He knew all the vocabulary on the list. Two students grabbed his paper, copying down the definitions in a frenzy. Michael spelled the words for me. It sounded so crunchy: "scoff."

He asked me if I knew what "laugh at" meant.

Yes. I know the word "laugh."

To laugh at someone is to scoff.

I memorized the word. I let other words slip by, and snatched up only another one, because of its four syllables: meticulous. I transliterated it into Lao.

The teacher, near the end of the period, gave me the same list of vocabulary and told Michael to tell me to look for definitions in the dictionary and learn them so I could take the next quiz. Each definition, I soon found out, led to more vocabulary words.

The second period followed. I tagged along with my cousin. I tended to panic and turn to Michael all the time for spelling, for interpreting, for help writing a sentence, always forcing my paper on him. I knew Americans valued independence, and I was weak and dependent. I looked forward to the last bell of the day.

I had too many words to memorize, and all day I fought with myself against forgetting the few words I'd learned. I felt more relaxed when, instead of more lessons, an election took place during the last period of the day. The black girl who said we would become pals was running for something. Others raised their hands and nominated some names. A golden-haired girl stood up and declared, I second the motion.

I knew the words "second" and "motion." But putting the two together? I stored the phrase in my head. I did not listen to anything else for the rest of the period.

Back at my uncle's house, my other cousins gathered in front of the TV in the living room. A girl wearing glasses held a bowl of ice cream with strawberries and fought with her brothers for a seat in front of the TV. A boy hollered at her and told her to sit on the couch. She refused. She wanted to sit right in front of the TV. So they fought.

The whole house became so hot, even though it was only April. The hills all turned dry and brown, drained of nurturing moisture. I went into Michael's room and sat down by the bed. In a corner were stacked a guitar and three tennis rackets. On the wall the poster of a sports car and a trophy. Why not take a walk?

I stepped down the stairs. Outside the open front door, Uncle Chao, already back from work, stood on the stoop with Michael, looking at the garden and evidently talking about it. All the houses in the subdivision looked new, the fledgling trees newly planted. Uncle Chao, as he talked, pointed at the pond, which also looked new, the lush lawn, the two maple trees, the willow, and the miniature bamboo bush.

If the garden were mine, I would want to add a stone path that cut across the pond, or add a small fountain just to listen to the trickle of water or raise some carp. I would get rid of the lawn, and grow some vegetables there.

Should I step up and join them? Uncle might not wish to be disturbed. If I joined them, what would I talk to them about, and in what language? Perhaps I could tell them about Nongkhai, about how hot it was—hotter than Milpitas. I would say, But no matter how hot it got, people always dressed up in public, not down. Nongkhai was hot. The whole of Thailand was hot. And to go anywhere men had to wear trousers. Kids could get away with wearing shorts in the refugee camp, but even they ran the risk of being pointed to if they showed up downtown wearing shorts. Uncle Chao would know that.

Someone was playing a piano. I returned to Michael's room. I heard characters talking on the television and the unanimous laughter from the faceless audience coming from the background, but my cousins did not laugh along.

When she returned home from work, Auntie Chao was sullen. She seemed to ignore her children and went about the house silently seething with anger. She did not speak to anyone, but when she did, her voice sounded like a holler. One of her daughters hung on to her sleeves, and I had the impression that she merely suffered the girl's presence and that she would have preferred to be by herself, until the red molten lava cooled and congealed.

At six, I saw no dinner. By seven, still no indication of cooking. At eight, finally, Aunt Chao went into the kitchen. At nine, my cousins parceled out bowls and silverware on the dining table. Without announcement, everyone gathered at the table, pulling chairs out. Sit, sit.

I decided to act bold and walk into the kitchen, because if I stayed in the living room and if my cousin had to fetch me, my aunt would think I carried an air of self-importance and superiority, that I expected to be waited on. But if I walked in without the proper announcement, wouldn't I appear too forward?

My aunt did not smile or speak, except a grunt to indicate that she had heard what the girl who held on to her sleeve whimpered to her. Michael told me to take a seat anywhere. Anywhere? The kids did not seem to notice or mind their mother's sullen looks and her angry silence.

I sat down gingerly and had reached for the chopsticks when all of them, the children, the parents, suddenly closed their eyes in unison, cupped their hands, and became quiet. Michael began to mumble rapidly, and, in his hunger, slurred over the words. As soon as he finished with a hasty amen, all of them, again in unison, picked up the chopsticks and forks and began to tackle the dishes.

I did not dare to slurp the way my cousins did. I might appear too at ease and hence forget my station. I ate slowly, more rice, and less meat and vegetables.

The Chao family, busily eating, talked briskly. What could I talk about? I could talk about the Iranian refugees I had seen in the Hong Kong airport. A group of them rushing past us as the guide led us to the terminal. I knew they were Iranian because of the news I'd read. But my aunt might not want to hear the account.

Finally she spoke. I turned to her but never caught her eyes. The dark clouds still sat on her eyebrows. I should probably not mind her. Madame Françoise, in the camp, after airing her disgruntlement and complaints, no matter how heated they might sound at the time, returned to her usual behavior the next day, just as my father predicted. She fixed meals. No sign of faces torn. This time I should overlook the reversal of my aunt's behavior too.

Right after they ate, the boys reconvened in front of the TV, while, caught off guard, I found myself still eating, again the last to finish. I needed to eat faster. I gulped down the last mouthful and just as I debated about what to do, the oldest girl helped her mother put the dishes into the dishwasher. The girl who had earlier eaten a bowl of ice cream ate some more of it. My aunt still didn't seem to see me as she went about the kitchen. I escaped to the living room and sat by the window to get some fresh air.

In the middle of the night, a nightmare shook me up. A tall, thin man in white—loose white shirt, flappy white pants—appeared next to me, and when I touched him—his body cold and hard as ice—he turned slowly around and eyed me with a bruised green face and red lips. His body began to stretch taller and taller, toward the ceiling, as he stared at me coldly.

I couldn't sleep, dreading school and the prospect of mingling with a group of strangers who looked like they wanted to start a fistfight, dreading to be in the midst of unintelligible talking, my mouth shut, and to be given the vocabulary, the fill-ins, the quiz.

I continued to act gingerly in the house. I wore the same pair of jeans to school, though I would have liked to wash them. I wanted to ask my aunt if I could use the washing machine, but when I saw the bed of molten lava glowing in her eyes, I was silent.

On Friday night my father showed up with a stranger, probably a relative of Lilian. I looked about me first, before telling my father I did not want to go to school anymore, not in Milpitas.

To my surprise—he nodded, but stated that he intended to stay in San Francisco with Lilian.

I sensed what this implied, but was so eager to escape from Milpitas that I didn't mind staying at Lilian's place or even living with her. I had left her apartment without saying farewell or thanks—I simply disappeared. Now I would have to act thick-skinned, and reappear at her door, and face her. I was prepared to brave the prospect of her weekend cooking parties, just as long as I could get out of my uncle's home that evening, and as long as my father would not arrange to have me stay with Uncle Chao again. The thought that I couldn't work and start on my independence weighed on me.

I told Uncle Chao I was going to San Francisco with my father for the weekend. I didn't say I would not come back. I would wait until I had missed a few days of school; then I would call my uncle.

It turned out that Uncle Chao did not even call to inquire when I didn't show up on Monday morning for school, or Tuesday morning, or Wednesday morning.

Not much to pack. I still wore the same pair of jeans I had worn over a week. Auntie Chao had gone out, conveniently sparing me from having to face her before I left.

Once again we entered the valley of lights. The stranger drove. Beads of light flickered in the night as the gust off the bay shook the branches of the trees.

The driver pointed out the airport. See that? The plane. The moving beads of light. Again I lost my sense of direction, not knowing that we were looking at Highway 101 from Highway 280 along the hill.

Driving into San Francisco, we felt the weather had become cooler. In fact, the fog had already covered and diffused through the city.

My father had the key to the apartment. We entered. The lamp in the living room cast a soft warm orange glow on the sofa and the vase of plastic flowers. Lilian must have gone to bed already. The room still had its distinct odor, the stuffiness which should smell familiar. The blanket still retained its foreign feel—the peony pattern and the butterflies forever flying, forever stationary. I pulled it up to my chin, and dozed off.

IN THE CHERRY ORCHARD

This must be the right road, I remember it, Lilian said. She drove into the parking lot of the U-Pick Orchard. It looked so nondescript from the outside that she had driven past it twice.

The three of us got out of the car. Leaving the parking lot and walking toward the orchard, I couldn't see how the owner could make any profit from the rows of trees that bore fruit only once a year, until we stood under one tree and saw the clusters of ripe cherries hidden behind the layers of leaves at the top branches, the trunk itself rounder than the girth of both my arms put together.

So much fruit from one tree alone. My father marveled at the quantity of overripe cherries that had dropped all over the ground.

Not to mention what the birds have eaten, Lilian added. And more still hide in the tree waiting to be plucked. She pointed.

Only then did the possibility of an immense harvest impress us.

Eager for reaping, we picked the tree next to the owner's house. The owner gave us buckets and, worrying that the cherries all around him would rot, pushed us to pick. He failed to notice my father's enthusiasm.

His steps bouncy, my father climbed up the ladder under the tree to discover what was hiding in the foliage. After years of eating canned cherries, he would finally see a real one, touch it, and put it in his mouth.

But Lilian warned him about the insecticide, the danger of putting poison into his mouth along with the juicy fruit. For us, the prospect of eating a real, fresh cherry had remained remote, at least in Laos, because of the unavailability of the fruit. The promise of this pleasure, which began with the picture on the can label and ended with the sight of ripeness, roused him and provided the motivation for the trip to the orchard. He had paid the price of leaving his home and crossing the Pacific Ocean, only to find out that the cherries had been sprayed with poison.

But of course Lilian did not mean to say that the orchard owner had, in fact, sprayed the trees. Lots of times, humans said what they didn't mean. If he had used the insecticide, the owner would have been less enthusiastic about thrusting the buckets in our hands. He would have warned us.

Lilian was simply making a casual remark and didn't intend it to be taken literally.

She proceeded to pluck what fruit she could from the lower branches of the tree, plucking those cherries she could reach on tiptoe. Then she walked around to survey the rest of the orchard. She went just far enough to find out if other trees had as many cherries as the one she had picked from. She then returned to report that most of the trees had been plucked clean. The remaining ones are not as big as the ones in the tree you're working on, she informed my father, who was stationed on the roof of the owner's house, plucking away.

Once he was back on the ground, he said, People go straight

into the orchard. They think they'll find the cherries in abundance there. They overlook this tree by the entrance. But it's exactly this tree that has the treasure. He couldn't stop smiling as he carried the two buckets to the hose nearby. He washed some, finally put one in his mouth. He urged me to try.

I didn't need the urging. The cherries tasted juicy and sweet, and we kept eating, choosing the big dark red ones to wash.

But they tasted so different that I began to doubt if what I'd had from the cans, back in Laos, were real cherries. No amount of cherries, not even the two bucketfuls my father brought to the orchard owner to weigh, could equal the taste of the canned ones my mother had opened on a summer afternoon years ago.

Lilian spent twenty dollars on the two bucketfuls.

On the way to the car, while sucking a cherry, I thought about how I was tagging along on my father's date, and how his flaunting his relationship with Lilian went against every rule I knew. If a son lacks discipline, it is the fault of the father; if the discipline is not strict, it is due to the sloth of the teacher. If I were to go on a date, would my father object? He would lecture me, telling me to wait until I became eighteen. And if I were to start dating despite his objection, I would do so with discretion and tact, if not in secret. But here, in the Bay Area, we were far from our moral center, far from the approval, intervention, or criticism of the townspeople. The best I could do was to suck on the cherry and pretend I didn't know what was going on. Like my father, I avoided confrontations.

After we left the orchard, we drove around to see if any apricot or peach orchards were open to the public too. I fell asleep in the car, and when I heard Lilian's laughter seemingly coming from afar, I slowly opened my eyes. We had already left Brentwood and were now heading for the Caldecott Tunnel.

Already late afternoon. People still drove with surfboards

strapped on the roof of their cars or sailboats towed behind them. The beach must be close by.

Have enough sleep? Lilian asked.

I said yes.

Hot weather makes people drowsy, my father said.

As if I didn't know it already.

It's hot only on this side of the bay, Lilian said. On the other side of the tunnel, right away you can tell it's cooler. You'll see.

Is that so? my father muttered.

We entered the tunnel. And once we emerged from it, we saw large patches of clouds in the sky, not the span of blue of a moment ago.

You're right. It's cooler here, my father exclaimed. You can tell right away.

Lilian smiled.

They talked about the cherries they'd picked. San Francisco looked dark and moody, no sun at all. We couldn't believe the same sky could change so fast.

Just like the difference between the outside and the inside of a person, Lilian commented.

The window feels cool, my father said.

We felt the wind whipping *whoop-whoop* against the car.

My father was so overcome with the drama of the weather. He repeated, Such a quick change in so short a time. This side so cool, the other side so hot.

By the time we passed through Golden Gate Park, the fog had taken possession of the land. Overcast. Misty. For days already, this weather, Lilian said. We put on the blue-striped winter jackets.

Once we reached the apartment, Lilian and my father began to wash the cherries in the kitchen. The phone rang. Lilian dried her hands on a towel and hurried to the living room. She picked up the phone. It's for you, Big Brother.

My father took the phone. He greeted Uncle Chao, I became nervous: I had not told Uncle I would not return to Milpitas.

My father nodded as he talked to Uncle, saying that an apartment would be ideal. Uncle Chao is helping us look for a home, my father told me later.

Uncle Chao became dear to me again. I would say thank you to him.

Shortly before sunset we left Lilian's place—this time for good, because from now on we would have our own apartment. Uncle Chao found it within a week of the phone call. I would no longer be a guest in other people's homes.

Lilian kept extending her hospitality to us, saying, If you have free time, come to San Francisco. My father nodded most eagerly. I had no intention of seeing her again, so I ignored her invitation. She exchanged a few pleasantries with Uncle Chao by the car in the driveway.

My father told me to thank Lilian for her hospitality. But I refused to work my tongue and make it sweet; I simply said good-bye and waved. Lilian stood beaming.

Uncle Chao drove us to a strange place, away from San Francisco, away from Chinatown. We crossed the Bay Bridge. At some point Uncle pointed out a structure to me: the Oakland Coliseum.

It was night. We reached our new home in San Jose only to find out that we would share a three-bedroom apartment with two Vietnamese men. My father readily agreed to the situation, while I couldn't get over the surprise mixed with deep disappointment and the feeling of being betrayed. I stared at Uncle Chao with my mouth open—as my lips began to tremble. I turned away.

We moved into the third bedroom.

In the low-income-housing complex, a Vietnamese family lived upstairs, across from them a Mexican family. Close to the apartment was the laundry room. My father checked it out and came back to tell me it was coin-operated.

One of our roommates, Mr. Pham, worked in a downtown grocery store, a Southeast Asian/Chinese market that had opened recently. A stocky man, he spent his mid-twenties working ten-hour days, stocking the meat and vegetable sections, lifting boxes and crates. Six days a week. He worked longer hours when the business began to boom, so that he spent practically all his time in the store and returned to the apartment only to sleep. Every day he would leave for work before anyone got up.

The other tenant turned out to be a headache for my father. A few weeks after moving in, my father asked the sleepy-eyed, unshaven Mr. Pham, who had just returned from work, if he knew that the other tenant had been bringing a woman to the apartment.

What can they be doing behind the closed door? my father asked, following Mr. Pham into the bathroom as the latter began to fling off his shirt, unbuckle his belt, and pull down his pants. My father didn't seem to notice and kept babbling. Bad, bad. He told Pham about his plan to move out if the other tenant kept up such indecent acts. Pham dropped his underwear and stepped into the bathtub.

I hardly saw the other tenant. Perhaps once every other day. Mostly I heard the door to the tenant's room open and close, footfalls light. Once, I had a glimpse of the woman, just the side view of her as she slipped into her man's room and closed the door behind her without a sound. In my room I didn't hear any talking, or any whisper, any laughter, or even a light cough.

Eventually Mr. Pham asked the tenant to move out because his boat-people relatives would soon be arriving and they needed a place to stay. But after the tenant moved out, we took the vacant room so that my father and I each had a room.

The weekend after we moved in, Uncle Chao came over with Michael. They brought chopsticks, spoons, two rice bowls, plates, and even a hot plate.

You can cook on it. Uncle Chao turned the turtle-sized object in his hand.

I stared at him: Of course the hot plate is used for cooking, but how will we cook if you don't bring any pots and pans? Didn't you say you would take care of everything?

I now knew that by taking people's word too literally, I made myself vulnerable. I remembered a saying: one's deed should match one's word, one's outside should be consistent with one's inside, a person should mean what he says and say what he means, instead of saying one thing and doing another.

Don't worry. Do one thing at a time, Uncle said.

If our stomachs can wait until the next time you bring a pot or a pan, I thought, but said nothing. Uncle Chao also brought a portable black-and-white TV set. He called me over, by the name he had dubbed me. Come over here, George. He waved.

I threw Michael a glance. I'm not George. Stop calling me George, I grumbled.

Or Joe, Michael added, smiling, amused, leaning on the wall with arms crossed.

I am not Joe either, I said. Stop that.

Come over here. Uncle Chao waved.

What is it?

He pointed at the television set and advised me that I should watch TV each morning—there was a program for kids.

I don't watch children's programs.

You can learn English from it. After a pause he pointed out, Don't bend forward to read too much.

I stared at him: When have you seen me bend forward to read?

Reading is bad for your eyes, Uncle Chao continued. Before I could protest, he switched the subject by announcing he had an errand to run. At the door he turned around. I'll come again some other time.

My father thanked him for the goods.

*   *   *

We liked to take walks after dinner, to explore the neighborhood. We passed the walnut orchard. It took up the whole block, an open field with a few houses along the street and a few rows of dry, old, dust-laden walnut trees.

At first I had mistaken the walnuts for young pears and had wondered why the pears would drop all over the ground without growing to maturity. One day, as I passed the orchard, on the way to the supermarket, something dropped on my head and startled me with a cracking pain. I thought someone, a thug or a naughty kid, had thrown a stone at me. The object rolled to a stop. I picked it up. It was a green fruit, a raw pear with a hard shell. I peeled off the skin and discovered a walnut.

Walnuts were rare in my hometown in Laos. I had tasted them only once, when Ahma bought a few from a trader. She taught me how to use a hammer to crack them. If I searched the entire town, I would not find any. So how did they happen to come to the hands of the trader? They were rarer than a sprig of peach blossom.

It amazed us that people in America did not take walks to facilitate their digestion.

Walking not only helped digestion, it also put us into a situation that forced us to talk to each other. I told my father about the places I had discovered: the Happy Hollow Park, Japanese Tea Garden, the Eastridge Shopping Center. I showed him the walnut tree, but withheld a certain detail. One Sunday morning, the walk took us past the orchard. The only people on the street, we turned right and passed the gas station, heading toward the overpass. We looked at Highway 101 beneath us. We walked on and came to a parking lot at the intersection of King and Story Road. Out of curiosity we went to the open-air market on the parking lot.

All the goods appeared to be used and discarded, barren of sentimental value. While my father picked up a lamp from a stall, turning it about, I bent down to leaf through the stack of old magazines and picture books. The Mexican vendor gave the price of the lamp.

The low price must have surprised and then delighted my father, for he began to scout the rest of the market with a sense of purpose. He bought an iron and a thick, heavy frying pan. The thought of the two of us carrying the used objects on foot back to the apartment, crossing the overpass and passing the orchard, where people could see us from their cars, dismayed me. As I watched my father carry the newly bought pan and iron, I didn't like us to be the only ones walking on the street while the rest of the city drove. It made us stand out and intensified the pressure on us to blend into the mass and to remain inconspicuous by doing what others all did.

I felt left behind as the cars zoomed by. I generalized my own feeling of abandonment into an observation about the pace of the world, the world forging ahead—a scientific discovery, a new technology, a new form of progress—the world going at full speed, too fast for those who didn't speak English. We lagged behind.

The following Sunday at ten—a week after our discovery of the flea market—my father was getting ready to leave the apartment.

I sat on the sofa watching cartoons. I'm not going back to the flea market, you can go alone, I said. Why did he buy so many cheap and dirty used goods? The handle of the pan had a chip in it. I couldn't help thinking about the pan: filled with unknown fingerprints and germs, the unknown hands using the iron to press who knew what kinds of clothes.

He countered, You need to get some exercise, or else your legs will wobble. I kept watching TV. He went to the set and turned it off. Then he told me in his threatening voice to take a walk.

Reluctantly I slipped on the sneakers I had bought in Nongkhai, Thailand. Once again, we walked.

At the flea market, my father found a pot in one of the

stalls. And while he bent over to examine it, I chanced upon a pair of roller skates. I recalled the woman I had seen roller-skating with fluidity and speed down the hilly streets of San Francisco. If the shoes weren't too big, I would have tried them on. Perhaps I could find a pair my size somewhere. So while my father searched for pots and pans, I searched for shoes with wheels. I didn't find any. Perhaps next time I would.

On the way back to the apartment, my steps quickened. I saw myself outstripping the cars, trucks, and vans with my roller skates purchased from the flea market. This time, as we crossed the overpass to the orchard, the traffic failed to stress me out with its speed and noise. Even as the cars left me behind, I didn't feel that the world was deserting us.

Through repeated trips, in addition to the iron, the frying pan, and the pot, my father bought one more pot, a chair, a worn lamp, clothes hangers, a toaster, and even two pairs of jeans. I didn't find any roller skates that fit me.

To make a better use of time as the world progressed, we came up with a new reason for taking a walk after dinner: grocery shopping. It was the perfect time for getting groceries, the sun setting and the breeze just beginning to stir. Taking a walk, then, assumed a utilitarian purpose.

Beyond the orchard, we turned left and crossed the street to the grocery store. I didn't have the desire to shop, my full stomach giving me the illusion that we would not get hungry the next day. We bought the usual: milk, grape juice, beef, a bakchoy. At the checkout counter, I saw copies of *Time* magazine, with boat people on the cover. I picked up a copy.

The clerk at the cash register said, You can use food stamps only for buying food. You have to pay cash for the magazine.

My father took out two dollars from his pocket.

Where did they come from, the two dollars? I blamed myself for wanting to read in English. I didn't have to use the magazine to learn how to read English.

On the street, my father said he wondered why all the prices in America ended in nine. Ninety-nine cents are actually $1.00; $9.99 is $10.00. The deceptive mind of American businessmen. They trick you into thinking the price is lower, but it's only one cent different. He sounded like he was exposing a fraud.

It had not occurred to me to question the dubiousness of nine. Now that he mentioned it, I began to notice that all the prices, without exception, ended with nine. Not to be tricked, I began adding one to them. Sometimes I even added a few more cents, to make the item appear overpriced so I would not be tempted to buy it. I aimed to outthink the crafty businessmen.

As we carried the groceries back to the apartment, the feeling that the city was driving past us and abandoning us returned. It was the load, the groceries in our arms, which slowed us down. The world went on at an ever faster pace, kicking up a screen of dust to obscure our faces, leaving us further behind. I felt unbearably forlorn.

The dust, the foul air, attacked us. My father was a firm believer in the vital importance of clean air. Each night he left the windows open. If he had a choice, he would sleep in the open air, under the moon. We didn't like to breathe in the dust, and the feeling of falling behind made us even more desperate.

We began to walk faster, hurrying until our heartbeats became loud and urgent. We broke into a sweat. The seconds ticked by.

As soon as we stepped into the apartment, I fetched the magazine from the grocery bag. I located the article on the boat people and began reading. Already I found raw words in the first sentence, and I wrote them down. I continued not so much to read as to seek out more strange words, listing them in a column. There was an article about a hit TV series called *Dallas*. It took another year before I became a fan. When I looked up from the magazine, the sky was still light, though it was past eight o'clock.

Meanwhile my father put the groceries into the refrigerator. He went to the bathroom, returned to the kitchen, began to rummage through the cabinet. Listing the raw words by the window, I heard the sound of plates and bowls. My father could have left them out to dry. He wiped them, put them back in the cabinet, and rearranged them. He spent a long time in the pantry. What could he possibly be doing? Why did he fold the plastic bags and brown bags?

In the morning I flipped on the TV, but found the children's program Uncle Chao had recommended boring. A big clumsy ostrich in a phony outfit wrote on a board. The ostrich turned its beak to the screen and began to speak in an old man's harsh voice. The beak opened and closed. The ostrich's voice sounded hoarse and scratchy, as if a fish bone had gotten stuck in its throat. I didn't see how I could learn English from this clunky ostrich. I changed the channel.

After watching TV, I took out the English-Chinese dictionary and began searching for the definitions of the raw words. I jotted them down. I picked out the words that I wanted to learn first and the ones I was most likely to use, choosing "intact" over "stalk," "efface" over "browbeat." My goal was to learn a few words a day, by memorizing the spelling and definitions. If I kept at it each day, I would know a few hundred words by the end of summer—I would be able to read.

INOCULATION

On the map: a tiny square with a stiff, triangular black banner on top, near the street I lived on. Scanning left, I saw another square with a banner, near the intersection of Story and King Road. Two schools for me to choose from. I looked at it again, the distance of the two symbols from the street I lived on, before folding up the map.

My father had left it to me to look for a school, because, he said with a helpless tone, he had his own concerns and worries.

I waited for the bus at the stop in front of the gas station.

The bus took me to King Road, where I got off. I walked toward the school, following the map. Although on the map the school looked to be right near the intersection, it took me more than twenty minutes to walk there from the bus stop.

Was this the right place? No sign. Just a fenced-in athletic field. Next to it were several basketball courts, all empty. Behind them stood a row of one-story buildings, the classrooms. No one was in sight. A small airplane landed at the airport next to the school. I saw no entrance. Maybe I could cross the field to check. I didn't want to trespass. Nor did I want to go around the street to the other side to check. I turned back, telling myself the other school might be better.

I waited until the next day to check out the second school. I didn't see the bus route on the map that would take me there. So I walked.

It had green lawns. Again the buildings were uniform, one story tall, with red tile roofs. I thought that in the U.S. every building would be multistoried. One-story buildings, like shacks, were for poor countries. Other than the few cars in the parking lot, the whole school was empty.

I heard birds as I crossed the parking lot toward the row of classrooms. I saw, ahead of me, an area with stone tables and benches. A building to my left had a row of tiny windows, all closed. They looked like ticket windows at movie theaters, with a semicircle at the bottom.

I went near the dark, opaque glass door to peek in. To my surprise the room was lighted and there were people typing, talking on the phone, scribbling at their desks. Who would have guessed that it was an office? I tried the doorknob and it turned. I entered.

The woman at the front desk asked how she might help me. I told her I needed to register for school.

In the next few sentences, she asked me if I had had a shot. Shoot, shot, shot. The shot? I glanced at her.

Have you had a shot? she again asked.

Trying not to feel embarrassed, I told her I didn't understand her. I wished she would keep her voice low. She mentioned the hospital. She played a nurse holding an imaginary syringe and giving an injection to her own arm.

So why didn't she just say injection? Why do I need it? I asked. I didn't want to risk the new word I'd just heard and so used "it." After I have "it," can I register then?

Hopefully, the woman said.

Another new word. Vaguely recognizable. Americans talk a lot about "hope." Where will I go get one?

She fetched a piece of paper from a folder and handed it to me. It tells you what to get and where to go.

Could I get there by bus? I only know buses 25 and 72.

Bus 25 will get you there, she told me.

The next day I set out for my "injection." I wore the pair of sneakers Uncle Chao had wanted me to throw away. On my way out I saw my father dozing off at the table, his English-lesson book open in front of him, a pair of nonprescription glasses (he had never gone to see an optometrist) on top of it. His cheeks were sunken, his lower jaw sharp, his chin pointed, his eyes bulging. Deep wrinkles on his face. He had never gained back the weight he lost in the refugee camp.

Why didn't he look for a job? I had asked him. We had been in San Jose for months. Need to learn English first, he said. This I could accept if he didn't always sit around lost in thought. Who learned anything that way? Sitting at the table, staring at the air. His eyes didn't seem to fix on anything, not on the floor or the table. Unaware of me, he began to snore.

He kept stalling. It occurred to me that he used his lack of English as an excuse, a pretext to shun contact with the out-side world, the bewildering English-speaking world, the world of foreign faces, the world that turned him into a deaf-mute. At this pace, napping instead of using every minute to memorize more raw words, when would he learn enough to speak? Did he want to eat welfare for the rest of his life? Did he come to America to retire? He acted like he was ready for it.

A strong impulse seized me—I wanted to scream in his ears or shake his shoulders. I slammed the door as I stepped out-side. That would wake him. Let him wonder where I went.

I had the map and the sheet of paper with me. I had checked the word "shot" in my bilingual dictionary. It had to do with immunization, shot. I crossed the street to the bus stop.

I passed the orchard, passed the tree where the walnut had dropped on my head. Someone handed me a walnut, already cracked open. I recognized my mother's hand.

Walnuts are hard to find, she said. She wore her hair the same way, the hairdo she gave herself. She had on her usual attire, the sleeveless blouse, the baggy pants tapered at the ankle. I looked like her, and was comforted by our resemblance.

Do they come from the north? I asked.

They disguise themselves as raw pears, to fool our eyes, and fool us into thinking they're rare. Eat it. Eat this one. She handed over the walnut she'd cracked. Eat it and hurry. The bus will arrive soon.

Standing under the dusty old walnut tree, she began to wave slowly. I blinked and she was already several trees farther away. Her hand blurred as she waved, the image fainter now. In the next instant she stood under the last tree of the row, at the end of the block, still waving. Then she disappeared.

The bus took me to an area where private homes had green, well-mowed front yards and tree-rimmed sidewalks. A world apart from my neighborhood. The bus approached a large building. Cars were parked there. More like a modern city. The sign read SANTA CLARA VALLEY MEDICAL CENTER.

The street where I would get off, according to the map, was still some distance away. The bus passed the medical center and entered busy streets where other buses were running and then onto a large, quiet street with shady, tree-lined sidewalks. This California street conjured up an image of a tree-lined thoroughfare in Vientiane, with three-wheel paddle cabs running leisurely along it, trees taller than the two-story shops. I would get off at this street. I pulled the string to signal for stop.

The address on the clinic and on the paper in my hand matched. I walked into the building and waited in line. I was directed to another room and waited in line over there. When my turn came, the nurse gave me papers to fill out. I told her I needed immunization for school. Using such a big word, "immunization," instead of "shot," made me feel grown-up and in control. I began to fill out the papers, and left blank the space for parental signature, wondering if I should sign my name there.

Finally, after filling out what I could, I told the nurse I didn't have my parent's signature. She asked how old I was. I told her.

Yes, we need a parent's signature before we can give you the shot.

My father can't come. He doesn't speak English.

She told me, in that case, to take the form home. I needed to come back with the signature. There was no other way.

Another waste of time! I burst out of the clinic, blindly brushing past people along the way.

That evening, I showed my father the form. He put on his glasses and held a pen and the form, but didn't know where to sign. His paralysis in front of any form—the papers from Social Security and MediCal, tax forms, consent forms, sweepstakes envelopes with his name on the label, the myriad questionnaires—infuriated me. But my father would shove the papers to me and expect me to deal with them. I could read most of the words, but didn't always understand what was required by the forms, what the content of them really meant. When I wouldn't—or couldn't—help him, my father seethed with anger.

I pointed to the appropriate box and he quickly signed.

I returned to the clinic the next day, had the shot, and had the immunization record filled out. Then I returned to the high school.

I presented the immunization record to the secretary who had told me that "hopefully," with the shot, I would be admitted. She checked the form, asked me what grade would I be in. I said nine. I wanted to go to high school and ninth grade was the lowest I would consider enrolling in. I would settle for ninth grade now because I planned to skip grade ten. It all depended on how hard I could work. Ninth grade, I told the secretary.

After checking the record for my age, the secretary shook her head.

We can't admit you, she said. You belong in grade eight.

I told her I wanted to go to high school. Eighth grade is too low for me. I even thought of going to grade twelve.

She returned the immunization record to me, shook her head, and spoke with finality. Come back when you're ready.

Did I have to wait—and waste—one more year? Had I not wasted enough time? This woman, who several days ago had assured me with the word "hopefully," now denied her word. I bit my lower lip. I wish you never said "hopefully." I raised my voice. I wish I never heard that word.

I threw the door open and bolted out. The school was still empty. A few seagulls perched on the picnic tables and benches. The red-brick buildings looked serene, the school that turned me away. School would begin after three days. Three more days.

I returned to the office and, fighting to control my voice, asked the woman where was the right school for me.

She gave me a long look before she fetched the address from a stack of papers, and as she gave me the directions, I felt deflated. If I couldn't attend high school, then I would rather not consider the alternative.

Instead of going to the school the secretary had indicated was the right one for me, I decided to return to the first high school, the one next to the small airport.

On the first day of school, when I saw my father about to leave the apartment to go to his language class, I said, You have to come with me. The school needs your signature for my registration.

He wore that kind of careworn look, full of hardship. I said,

You can just sign your name. I will do the talking. His expression made me feel that I was making his life harder and wearing him out. I know you have to sacrifice your time and cut your class. Would you rather that I do not go to school? Would you want that? Is your school more important, or mine? No answer. I cursed the school for coming up with so many rules. Signature, signature, everything needs a signature. And when I saw him still not getting dressed, I screamed it's almost eight! The class will have already started by the time we get there. Hurry up. Do you hear? Hurry!

He tucked his shirt into his pants. I tore at my hair, pacing frantically back and forth in the living room. I hated him for keeping us in such a dependent position. My father tied his shoes. I wish I didn't have to go to school, I yelled. I wish I could get a job!

I slammed the door as we left the apartment.

On the way to the bus stop, I saw orange school buses full of students drive by. Here I am, on the first day of school, without a school to go to, I grumbled. We trudged along. The bus was packed with students standing up, holding the bar in the aisle. Some students, knapsacks strapped on their backs, wore uniforms. We got on and squeezed through the aisle. Faces looked at us strangely. Voices so loud. I reminded myself to keep my balance in case the bus braked suddenly.

After getting off, I chose the street where I assumed the school entrance would be. Approaching the school, I heard the bell. Students ran. No matter where they were, whether in the refugee camp or here in San Jose, students behaved in the same way, racing and yelling instead of walking quietly.

I spotted someone who looked like a teacher patrolling the hallway. I went up to her. First I said excuse me. I told her I was looking for the office to register. Only to be told, in the office, that because of my address, I belonged to another school district. We cannot take you. You will need to go to the school in the school district you belong in.

This was another new concept, the school district. It goes against my notion of freedom, I felt like telling the secretary. Why can't I go to the school I want to go to?

I rushed out, leaving my father in the office. I wanted to run, if only to breathe more easily. But I checked this impulse and shuffled rapidly instead. My chest felt compressed.

My father looked puzzled, his mouth slightly open. He stepped out of the office. Instead of following my headlong pace, he walked slowly, with arms crossed. His steps took on a kind of meditativeness.

I charged down the street, flourishing my arms, yelling. I'm not going to school. You can go to yours. I'll stay in, and if a gang or secret society will take me, I'll gladly join. Gladly! I'll wear long hair. Grow a mustache. Smoke cigarettes. Talk dirty. Look mean at all ladies and gentlemen. Again I tore at my hair, messing it up.

My father trudged behind me.

That night, I checked the definition for "intermediate," and as I closed the dictionary, I sighed, resigned to my demotion to a lower grade.

At seven the next morning, my father and I walked to the "intermediate" school, the one located at the address the secretary had given me, just a block and a half away from the apartment.

I presented the immunization record at the office, and after signing the papers, my father hurried off to his language class.

I was led without further trouble or delay to my class. The two teachers introduced themselves as Mrs. Caulfield and Mr. Vasquez. They said they started this class just for the new students who couldn't speak English.

Couldn't speak English? I knew the alphabet and I didn't intend to learn it again with the beginners.

The teachers told the class we were special. Mrs. Caulfield wrote on the board three big letters and then beneath it she wrote, ENGLISH AS A SECOND LANGUAGE.

There were few students, about twenty. Lots of empty

chairs. Half the class spoke Spanish. The other half spoke Vietnamese. There was one Korean. No other Lao or Chinese. Over the next few weeks, new students arrived almost daily. New faces, with large inquiring eyes, showed up at the door. Among them was an Iranian student, called John. I kept waiting for a Lao or Chinese to walk through the door.

ROLLER SKATING

With a list of raw words, such as "rock" and what seemed to be a synonym, "rolling stone," and "disco," Mr. Vasquez introduced us to the world of music. Finally, I knew what "Bee Gee" meant. Very popular, Mr. Vasquez said. He flashed a photo of the Bee Gees from his wallet and paraded in front of the class, raising the photo in the air.

The Iranian student raised his hand.

Do you have a question, John?

John asked Mr. Vasquez if he carried the photograph in the wallet with him all the time. Mr. Vasquez nodded.

John said, I don't believe it.

Mr. Vasquez cast a look at Mrs. Caulfield at her desk. She smiled, stood up, and told the class that Mr. Vasquez was a big fan of the Bee Gees. She asked if we knew what a "fan" was, then proceeded to explain the term.

Mr. Vasquez took out more photos from his wallet. One of them was a photo of Robert Redford. Mrs. Caulfield said, Mr. Vasquez is a big fan of Robert Redford too.

I carry the photos with me every day, confirmed Mr. Vasquez.

Everywhere you go? John looked incredulous.

Everywhere I go, John. Mr. Vasquez then took out some money from his wallet to show it to the class. He then showed his driver's license, his credit cards, and the stack of celebrity photos, raising them in the air as he walked back and forth in front of the class. The class laughed.

Mr. Vasquez closed his wallet. From a box on his desk he took out a T-shirt with a silkscreen of a rock group and the word KISS in sharp angular letters. The group had painted, scary faces. Mrs. Caulfield said Mr. Vasquez got the T-shirt from a rock concert he went to ("concert" was on the list). She then passed out a short article about the rock group. And Mr. Vasquez gave the class a crossword puzzle to work on, using all the vocabulary on the list.

One day Mrs. Caulfield announced to the class that I would have a new friend. She said from now on I would have someone to speak Laotian to, but only outside class.

During the recess, in the playground, Somseng, the new student from Laos, told me in English that his parents could speak Lao. He asked me, Do you know Hmong?

Of course not. I was a lowlander. I conveyed this with a blank stare. I assumed the new student would know. We spoke in simple English.

After the recess, Mrs. Caulfield asked me what did I find out about my new friend, whether we spoke Laotian to each other. I told her the new student was Hmong and he knew only two Lao words, "yes" and "no"; his favorite gestures included nodding and shaking his head, and he smiled plenty, revealing his dimples. I wish he speaks some Lao, I told Mrs. Caulfield.

Later I found out that this Hmong student had become Christian. On Friday afternoons, before the last class ended, he would invite me over for the weekend so we could go to church.

Come. He reached for my hand.

What are you doing? Boys don't hold hands here. I drew away.

He blushed.

I thought about inviting him too, to befriend him, simply because we came from the same country. But I soon realized his idea of fun was to talk about God and the Big Book. Sometimes he carried a pocket-sized version of it to school to show me during lunch break and offered to lend it to me.

I told him I was Buddhist. I believed in karma. But more importantly, changing one's faith represented an act of betrayal.

He didn't seem to hear me, and kept talking about the Book, pushing it into my hand. I felt so bored that I started to regret my friendly overtures.

Every day I saw the camaraderie among the Spanish-speaking students and among the Vietnamese students. They had so much to relate to each other, chatted and joked so easily in their own language. Even though they were new to the U.S. and new to the school, they were so at ease, because they had their fellow countrymen around them.

At the sight of them talking among themselves, I would feel left out. I became quiet, and yearned for the same kind of relaxed, natural companionship. This led me to seek out Somseng, even though I knew he tended to talk about the Big Book all the time and never tired of trying to convert me. It never failed. We would start talking and within a minute I got so fed up I wanted to shut my ears or say, You should be ashamed of yourself, giving up Buddhism. How could you change so fast, becoming a Christian just so you could come to this country? I knew this would hurt Somseng's feelings, or embarrass him. The Hmongs fought for the U.S. during the war. They were loyal soldiers. Plus, I doubted if Somseng had been a Buddhist before. I had not seen Hmongs going to temples, not in Laos or in the refugee camp.

During recess one morning, I went up to Mrs. Caulfield and, in passing, mentioned that Somseng spoke good English. He should be transferred, I added.

He might know how to speak English, but he still needs to learn reading and writing, said Mrs. Caulfield.

ESL is too easy for him, I said.

How do you know?

He speaks English, I said.

Yes, but not well enough.

You don't think his English is good?

Mrs. Caulfield didn't think Somseng knew enough English to be in a regular class. And in a confiding tone she said, He still has plenty to work on. Don't worry. We'll keep him busy. As she said this, Mrs. Caulfield passed a glance and a smile to Mr. Vasquez.

I know what roller skate is, I told John, who was seated across from me.

Then how come you don't know how to skate?

I never try it.

I don't believe you. Everyone knows how.

Not me. I don't know how.

If you don't know how to roller-skate, you don't get to go to the field trip. John then turned to the Korean student. You know how to skate, Song?

Song nodded. He came across as being quiet because, I bet, of his limited English. John, Song, Somseng, and I were among the few students who had to speak English to each other, even during recess, whereas the rest of the class would speak in Spanish or Vietnamese.

I don't believe you. You lie. John pushed my shoulder.

John, if you don't shut up, I'm going to tell everyone you're Iranian. I had just learned the word "shut up" and tended to use it whenever I could.

Nooo, John protested, and reached across the seat to grab

me. No, don't tell anyone. But everyone in the class already knew.

I'm going to tell.

Don't. He looked miserable.

I will, if you don't stop.

John quieted down. He was afraid of getting harassed by American students from the regular class: the situation of American hostages in Iran appeared on TV every day. After a minute, John tapped my shoulder. Promise me.

Promise you what? Annoyed, I raised my voice.

Promise me you will not tell.

John, will you stop, will you?

When John had first come to the class, in order to get to know him, I told him about what I had seen in the Hong Kong airport. On the way to the U.S. we had stayed overnight in Hong Kong before catching the plane the next morning. We were following the guide to the departure gate when we saw a group of refugees coming toward us. The two groups hurried past each other. And I recognized the other group as Iranians because I had heard the news and recognized my own reflection on those people's harrowed faces. I knew they had left their country and were going to a different one. In transit.

Yes, people were leaving the country, John said. Like his family.

The inside was dark. Dots of pink and blue lights coursed around in circles as we burst into the skating rink.

Come on. John couldn't wait to slide into the ring.

I hurriedly put on the roller skates, which felt at once heavy and slippery, a kind of leaden slipperiness. Somseng started to move slowly, testing his balance. I groped for the floor, sprawled on all fours, screeched. A group of Latino girls groped along the wall. John the roller skater milled comfortably among others. Mr. Vasquez was nowhere to be found.

A few practiced outside the ring, where people went to rest. A blond couple flitted past the group, zipping smoothly around the rink. In a moment they flashed past the same group again. Someone in the group fell down, causing others to follow suit. John was coming up from behind and he could have bypassed the trouble spot, but instead he headed right into it, his hands stretched out, his eyes fixed directly on the people who were trying to get up from the slippery floor, and then he smashed right into them.

Meanwhile the couple coursed through the rink, with the wheel of blue and red dots of light circling the ceiling and the walls, disco music blaring. The blond boy let go of the blond girl's waist and began to slide backward, as if sucked into a vacuum. But just as fast, the girl sped ahead. It looked as if he were going to smash into her any moment now as he skated backward with such mad, blind speed, apparently unaware that she was coming up from behind. But as if he could see out the back of his head, all at once he whipped around and grabbed the girl by the waist. Once again they moved in the same direction. It looked like such fun.

I too wanted to have fun. I stood up, and summoned my courage. By then the girls—my classmates—were moving tentatively along the side of the ring. I stepped into the ring, groping for the wall. The girls wouldn't move along and my roller skates skidded ahead, out of my control. I screeched, reaching for Somseng.

Don't—don't touch me, he cried out. He fought to shake me off. Too late: the girls looked stunned as they watched me skidding madly toward them from across the ring. I buckled and fell with a loud *plop*, and even before I reached them, they buckled too. Their loud scream ensued. All groped around trying to scramble up as a train of skaters approached and, unable to bypass the tangled mass on the floor, smashed into us. More screams. The blond couple flowed past, unseeing. Then I saw Mr. Vasquez floating like a heavy swan, keeping a safe distance from the mass on the floor. The heavy swan made a face at us as he glided smoothly on his wheels.

I managed a few shaky turns around the ring. My knees and elbows hurt. But it was worth the pain.

During the Thanksgiving holiday, Song suggested that we—he and Somseng and John and I—go roller skating. We had gone back to the rink a few times since the field trip.

We got off bus 72 and waited at an intersection to transfer to a second bus. The bus stop was under a big old tree. Behind the tree and parallel to a power line ran a railroad track, and beyond that was an open field, like that in a countryside. But just across the busy street were a supermarket, a gas station, a fast-food restaurant, all decorated for Christmas, and a parking lot full of cars. It already seemed dark, even though it was only early afternoon.

We waited for the bus quietly. Speaking English tired us. Too much exertion of our jaws and tongues, as though we were still unused to the texture of this new kind of food in our mouths. Of course the ability to speak a new language, even just a handful of sentences, inspired a secret joy in us. There were times when our tongues were itchy, tempted to try it out. But after working our jaws and tongues with great vigor—because that's what the language required—the strain would spread from that region of our bodies to somewhere deeper, so deep that we had to sigh to relieve it.

Because we couldn't speak to each other in our native tongues, and because we found speaking English more uncomfortable than being quiet, we played mute. Below the tree, I peered at Song. He looked at the ground, meditative. Somseng gazed at the sky, perhaps in communion with a higher being. Squatting, elbows to knees, John had a pensive air. Hands in my pockets, I leaned on the tree and looked far ahead, toward the open field.

Roller skating, it turned out, dispelled the strain of speaking English. Motion quickened our heartbeats. We became alive and monkeyish, with small gestures and movements. There were only a few people in the ring. I stepped in. Now I could manage one round without falling—just as long as I let the rollers carry me and didn't pause to think what my legs were doing. Who could resist the urge to increase the speed? With such a heightened, exhilarated feeling, it was no wonder the skillful skaters couldn't help but turn, skate backward, perform some stunts, or dance along.

When we rested, we began to perspire. Song said something. The DJ was playing a song by Michael Jackson. What? I yelled. I can't hear you. With roller skates on, we stood by the side, ready to get in again. We grabbed the moment and burst into the skating ring.

THE WEDDING

Pham came into the living room and asked me how I had spent the day. I told him I went roller skating. After a brief chat, he then—catching me unawares—told me to be nice to my father. Surely he was insinuating that he was aware of my lack of respect? My ears pricked up.

He needs a wife, Pham said.

I turned a sharp glance at Pham, who had nothing better to do than to take on the banal role of the matchmaker. So nakedly bold! People's strong impulse and zeal for match-making must be innate, I thought. By this time the innate human compulsion to matchmake had been plentifully rein-forced in my mind.

He's a good father, Pham told me.

This notion, on the other hand, required reinforcement. I puckered my mouth.

It's for your own good—your new mother can cook for you.

For my own good? I would keep this in mind.

My father disliked cooking. He simply tossed whatever he had at hand into the wok, kept the fire strong. And he usually burned the pot when he was cooking rice, until he began using Pham's rice cooker.

He's good to you, Pham repeated.

I felt a rush of moisture in my eyes. I remained stony. Just then I heard the sound of a key turning the lock.

The door opened and my father stepped in with a bag of groceries in his arms. Woh! So cold outside. He stamped on the mat behind the door a few times.

My father and Pham—could they have planned this, timed my father's entrance? My father would step out of the apartment on purpose so Pham could convey his message. After a few words to soften my ear, this outsider, the roommate turned fox had then had the insolence to tell me to behave.

Go shopping? Pham stood up from the chair.

Yeah.

I wondered how my father had picked up the word "yeah." His other favorite was "mmm-hmm." Did he learn them at his language class? Did his instructor have him practice saying things like mmm-hmm and uh-huh?

He put the groceries into the refrigerator.

My father often lapsed into gloom, sighing and grumbling about lacking the certificate that was required for a job application. He blamed what he called "moldy luck."

How could he blame bad luck? When our neighbors had begun to flee Laos, my father refused to make plans for us, content to stay—cowering—in the backwater of the world, instead of venturing to America or Europe. Uncle Chao's words echoed in my head: They need carpenters over there. The husbands—tailors, ex-soldiers, traders, some with minimal skills, but men of vision and courage—led their families across the Mekong to the refugee camp in Thailand, in search of a better life abroad, while my father continued to go about his daily routines, unconcerned for our future, taking orders from the Comrades.

He spent much of his time alone. He had never before struck me as the solitary type. On the contrary, he was the one with the three-foot tongue, from which his speech flowed like a waterfall. To court and woo Lilian, for instance. But life in America had forced him into solitude, changed him. Denied him friends. The waterfall had lost its splendor. Boulders in the form of the English words that were so difficult for him to grasp now impeded the flow.

And this was a man who liked to sing! Didn't he surprise me in Ohio by singing poetry? In Laos, after spending a day doing communal work for the Comrades, he would return home, hang his tank top on a clothesline, and head off to wash himself in cold water, singing "The Green Island Serenade." He would make his voice gruff and throaty, belting out, *This Green Island, like a boat, swings and sways in the night, but why do you sway and drift . . . ?*

Because he had such a hard time learning English, I knew it was impossible for him to get a carpenter's license. He would fail the examination, time and time again. But I knew he could do the job, and do it well. He knew how to repair a roof, fix plumbing, install lights and windows. All of which required no English. I was angry for him, angry with the inflexibility of the establishment. The immediate future looked bleak.

He was fifty years old, yet I expected him to be strong, to challenge the world, to conquer it. From the way he sat by the table staring blankly at the floor, he looked anything but strong. Employers not only looked for someone who could speak English, they also preferred someone young and energetic.

He sat by the table feeling depressed, useless, shut in, hopeless. His cheeks caved in, his eyes became hollow and lusterless. He stared at his hands. How much longer could he go on like this?

He wondered whether he was closer to death than to a job. In despair, the prospect of death began to gain appeal. It brought calm to his mind. Which in turn made the actuality of unemployment less nerve-racking.

Just then he thought of Lilian. His mind made a struggle, resisting the thought of suicide. He sat straight. Lilian was what he could look forward to. He still had her. He must get married, and start a family, job or no job. It became his way out, getting married.

Pham and my father began talking in the living room after my father put the groceries in the refrigerator. I closed my bedroom door and dropped into bed. I felt bitter as I slowly came to realize the fragility of human love. Three years after my mother's death, he was ready to replace her.

Mother frowns, her eyebrows in a knot. It stays with her. She does not talk. She has been this way in my dreams.

I wanted to find her. I studied my gaze and saw her somewhere in my eyes. I smiled and saw her somewhere at the corners of my lips. The eyes smiled back at me. I was looking more and more like my mother.

When I was by myself, she was in my silence, just the way I used to see her sitting by herself in her hair parlor, in silence.

As for my sister, my impression of her in the dream would be rapidly receding as I woke up. The flickering image of her gaze seemed harder and harder to capture, her bright laugh less and less audible, her sprightly prance more and more distant.

My mother must have been frustrated with my father, disappointed in him, having seen through him. She must have seriously considered leaving home with or without him when she wrote that she would "contact" me in the refugee camp in Ubon, Thailand. I had assumed that "contact" meant she would write to me again, soon. What she really meant, it now appeared, was that she intended to come join me. She added the phrase not only to comfort me but also to confirm her decision in her own mind.

Having heard the rumor that the Comrades intercepted all letters coming into as well as those going out of the country, she advised me to be discreet in my letters. Which meant my first two letters had reached her. Then I didn't hear from her for about two months. Perhaps the Comrades had confiscated her letters.

My mother set out to cross the Mekong because she did not want to be like her husband, who talked big without action. He said she overworried and assured her I was safe in Thailand. She had believed him for a while, and whenever she felt disappointed with him, with his empty prattle, she told herself she should have known better than to take him seriously, to entrust him with her and her children's lives.

He went to see Lilian on the following weekend. He proposed to her. Wasn't my answer already implicit? She smiled. She wanted to consult a monk in order to learn the most auspicious date for the wedding. She would want to have three, perhaps four kids, she told him. He too wanted to have many children. He tried not to let his job situation dampen his spirits. So even though he told Lilian he wanted many kids, he had decided that he really wanted no more than one.

My mother got angry first with him and then with herself. She cloistered herself in the bedroom, hoping he would see her raging silently and know why. At night, she turned her back to him as soon as he got into bed—after his nightly visit to the teahouse, for I knew my father frequented the teahouse often and stayed until quite late. He had no sense, she realized. The neighbors, and those of her friends whose husbands were able and sensible, had fled the country.

She did not pretend to be asleep, her eyes open. She had let her seven-year-old daughter sleep in the middle of the bed, between her and her husband. Soon he began to snore. She blocked her ears.

That night, after she accepted his proposal, they went to bed. Lying next to him, Lilian felt comforted. They had been through a lot together, she thought. On the morning of the day she left the camp to go to America, she told him she would wait for him in America. It was only a short separation, she comforted him. She felt strong, setting out for a strange land on her own. And one day he would join her there. They would go to see Golden Gate Bridge together, take a picture there. She landed in San Francisco. She couldn't describe how frightened she was, once she arrived in America, how bewildering it was, and how lonely. A refugee agency found her a clerical job in a bank. After work she went to see movies by herself, reluctant to return to the apartment where the hallway was half-lighted and smelled, where she often found cockroaches under her bed, not to mention in the kitchen and the bathroom.

In bed, she let out a sigh of relief. She had put those days behind her. He snored next to her. I will have to get used to this sound, she thought, and then giggled. The day to see Golden Gate Bridge together had finally come.

My mother began to find more and more fault with him, to the point where she felt like bursting from the house and fleeing from the town. Her chest heaved unevenly, her face screwed up tight. She fretted, became easily provoked, when spoken to, lost her temper. Surely he sensed her discontent? Surely he would act?

Then came the news of the king's dethronement, which sent a quake through the town. Referred to in the old tourist manuals as the sleepiest town on earth, Luang Prabang seemed destined for permanent slumber. Half the inhabitants had fled to France and refugee camps in Thailand, leaving behind almost total stillness. The market looked empty. All the tailor shops were closed. If she waited, my mother too would become still, inert, drowned with the town in its sleep.

She thought about her brother in the U.S. She could always rely on him. Her brother had guaranteed that she would find a good life in America. But when she did not hear from him, she began to believe he had forgotten her. She had not counted on the change that time and distance would cause, the change on the part of her brother. Out of sight, out of mind. She realized this too late.

He telephoned the Chaos. He told his former brother-in-law he would marry soon. Would he do him the honor of attending the wedding?

Uncle Chao at first thought my father was asking him to be his best man, and then realized my father was inviting him as a guest. He was so busy these days he didn't feel like helping anybody or giving somebody the honor of doing something for nothing. Everyone for himself, was his motto. Plus, he had done enough for his poor relations.

My mother would not wait and remain idle if her husband continued to stall. The time had come to take charge of her life, just as if her husband no longer had anything to do with her life. This thought made her bitter.

She decided she would act without telling him. She tried not to get carried away, but the more she thought about me, and about her brother, Uncle Chao, in the U.S., who would sponsor her once she reached Thailand, the less patient she was with waiting and stalling. The urge to act possessed her. She would make some inquiries. People like Mrs. Lee would know how one escaped to Thailand.

I overheard my father telling Lilian on the phone to buy me a camera. His voice sounded as cajoling as ever. His speech, which I had likened to a dry waterfall, was in fact still inexhaustible, and now the flow renewed. Down the Mekong. A body rolled in the muddy current.

He dared not breathe a word to the Pathet Lao, or enlist their help to search for my mother and sister, adrift in the Mekong. I supposed he had found out where the boatman lived. The boatman's wife returned some of my mother's jewelry to my father, according to Ahma. Before starting out, the boatman had told the wives to give their valuables to him, in case on their way across the border they ran into the Pathet Lao, who would no doubt confiscate them. But once they were in the boat, the wives asked the boatman to give their jewelry back. Instead he beat them and sank the boat.

Where is he? my father asked the boatman's wife as she stood in the doorway. She returned my mother's gold and jade rings and said that the murderer had fled to Thailand. She flatly denied any responsibility.

I had no use for a camera, and if he presented me with one I would turn it down. But during the next week or two, I didn't see any camera, or any other bribe. Instead he broached the subject of his forthcoming marriage. I felt the inevitability of it as I listened. I mentioned his priority: to get a job. He told me not to worry about him. Concentrate on your school, he said, overriding my weak protest.

No, my father did not go to the boatman's house by himself. More than likely, he hurried there with the other bereft husbands. If they had not pressured the boatman's wife to reveal her husband's whereabouts, she would have kept all the jewelry. In the end, she grudgingly returned some.

A new task awaited my father: to bury my seven-year-old sister. But the best coffin he could build would do no good. He would ship the body back to our home in Luang Prabang. He was not alone. Other widowers and fathers too had to find coffins for the bodies that had been salvaged from the Mekong and ship them back home.

I have already made up my guest list, Lilian told him. I will invite my coworkers, the new friends I made, and the people from the refugee resettlement center. Oh, I will invite the Russian neighbor downstairs too; otherwise the wedding will be too noisy for her. Your task, she told him, is to give me a list of guests you want to invite.

They lay in bed. The time was three in the morning. Both firm believers in the vital importance of fresh air, they had kept the window slightly open to let in the freshest air of all, the cold ocean air. The window blind billowed. Under the street light, fog and mist came flying in from the ocean.

The new task awaited him, but other than his former brother- and sister-in-law and his roommate, he had no one else to invite. The thought of his good friends who had resettled in France, who had refused him aid when he was in the refugee camp, made him bitter and angry. Even Lilian sensed it. She asked him what was the matter. His list of guests was a blank.

How about your sister Karen?

I will send her an invitation, but I don't expect her to fly out here, he said.

Lilian, after a moment of silence, said that for the wedding she would serve the guests some Lao food, the dishes that she had a craving for. There were so many of them, though. She would have to narrow her choices.

She heard the foghorn. She liked that sound, liked listening to it at three in the morning.

He scheduled the wedding for a Saturday. I had no excuse not to attend it. I had to go, bear it, live with it. He had forced his mealtime arrangement with Madame Françoise on me before; he would do a similar thing again, without asking if it was the kind of household I wanted. I had long since figured out why he hadn't let me confront Madame about causing Ahma's death. It was because he owed Madame his gratitude for introducing Lilian to him. How could he accuse Madame of causing Ahma to suffer a stroke? I had no choice and no say.

He talked to Lilian on the phone. The word "band" kept coming up. Apparently Lilian insisted on having a band play for the wedding, which my father thought unnecessary and impractical.

I shut myself in the bedroom. I turned on the tape recorder. When the song came on, I pictured the singer standing on the Thai side of the Mekong, sending the song across the river.

In a few weeks we would be leaving the camp for America. Father said I needed new shoes. We went to see Ahma's tomb, in a temple outside the refugee camp, near downtown Nongkhai. In the temple yard, Father used a stick to brush away the leaves that had fallen in front of the tomb.

Afterward we went downtown on foot. We stopped by a jewelry shop. From his pocket my father took out a small purse that Ahma had put her jewelry in. From the purse he took out the pair of gold bracelets my sister had worn. They must have been on her wrists when my father found her body.

I'm comfortable in the shoes I'm wearing, I said. I peered at my toes through my sandals. They still fit me. I have no need for new ones, I said.

But he went ahead and sold the bracelets. He then took me to a shoe shop.

I didn't want new shoes.

On the morning of the wedding, I wore my usual clothing: jeans, a long-sleeved shirt, and the pair of sneakers my father had bought in downtown Nongkhai. It was the only pair of shoes I had. Ahma made sure my shirt and schoolboy shorts were tidy. She tied my shoes before she went out to flag down a three-wheel paddle cab.

Uncle and Auntie Chao picked me up and drove me to San Francisco. Uncle wore a suit and tie, and Auntie also dressed appropriately. They did not comment on my shoes, the pair they had wanted me to throw away. Ahma wore her usual white blouse and black silk pants.

Uncle took Highway 280. Because it has less traffic, he said. I wished the traffic would make us miss the wedding. After an hour or so we arrived in San Francisco. Uncle parked on Stanyan Street, next to Golden Gate Park. We crossed the street to the row of Victorian houses.

The paddle cab pulled to a stop in front of the hospital known for its French architecture, with a row of betel-nut trees in front. Ahma and I got out of the pedicab. Ahma, holding my hand, led me up the steps of the hospital. Mother lay in a hospital bed. She looked pale. She had just had a long surgery in order to deliver a baby and lost a large amount of blood. My father was giving her a blood transfusion: blood in a plastic tube went from his arm on one bed to hers on the other bed. I came to Mother's bedside to show her my report card. I told her about my grades. She smiled. Ahma said that my mother needed to rest, and that in the meantime she would take me to see my baby sister.

Uncle rang the apartment doorbell while Auntie held the wedding gift. I stood behind them. I could make out what the gift was. A woman in a pink dress, no doubt the bride's helper, opened the door. Her smile narrowed her eyes. She greeted us. Come in. Come in and have a seat. We walked into the narrow hallway. Come this way. Ahma led me down the hall. I shuffled along. We stepped into a ward where there were two rows of baby beds. We walked down the row; then Ahma stopped in front of a bed. In it was a baby with a tube attached to her nose. Ahma said that was my little sister.

The woman led us into the living room. I didn't know any

of the guests who crowded around there. They spoke in Chinese, Lao, and English. I looked at them, they looked at me. They couldn't have known who I was; for all they cared, my father was an old bachelor getting married for the first time. I sat on the sofa and wondered where the bride was. I had not been to Lilian's new apartment before.

I saw my father greeting the guests across the room. A happy groom, despite the uncertainty of his future. In a few months she would be able to smile, Ahma said. I stepped up for a closer look. My baby sister was almost hairless, her eyes shut tight, her face peach red. My father wore a *complet* and a *cravate* (pronounced "gar-ra-vat" as transliterated from French to Lao). Where did he get the suit? He looked so different, so presentable, standing there talking to the guests.

I wondered what the matchmakers in the refugee camp would say if they could see him now. Under the weak incandescent light in the hut, Ahma turned away from me, looked down, and whispered, as if she were afraid that her breath would blow away the particles on the table, Coming back? Returning? He's here. She patted my hand. He's with us now. Two praying mantes crawled slowly up the bamboo pole. I could see the perspiring face of Madame Françoise. I will go to your wedding, even if I have to crawl to get there, she barked. The glasses clinked and clanked as she toasted my father. Lilian the bride wore a serene expression of joy.

My father came over. I stood next to Uncle Chao. You've arrived, the groom said to me. I simply nodded, without saying congratulations. He and Uncle, the two former brothers-in-law, exchanged pleasantries. Uncle Chao appeared not to bear any harsh feelings toward my father, my father not to harbor any guilty feelings toward Uncle. Big Brother will make lots of money in California, Uncle Chao told my mother, who sat smiling, listening to her brother. I ate candies and listened to Uncle. Come to California, Big Brother. Uncle Chao patted my father's back. I didn't understand how Uncle Chao could watch his sister be replaced and still act so friendly. Neither man looked awkward or uncomfortable. In fact, they looked sharp in their suits and ties.

As I sucked on a candy, I studied the decor of the Victorian apartment, the flower patterns on the drapes, the ceiling corners—the guests' faces and clothes. Two praying mantes crawling slowly up the bamboo pole. I parted the drapes to glance at the springtime outside: all that activity in Golden Gate Park, the sunny sky, joggers with their Walkmans passing the stretch of tall eucalyptus. As I looked outside the window, a roller skater glided past right below it, the rollers crunching on the sidewalk. She turned around and waved. In a second she was already far away. Under the row of walnut trees, she waved.

When I caught sight of my father again, he stood with the bride greeting the guests and accepting their congratulations. Didn't I tell you I would crawl my way here? Madame Françoise teased the groom. At one point during the time in the camp, she had turned against her masterwork, ripped his face: when she sat in the doorway of the hut that early evening, scolding the widower for complaining about her cooking, it was nothing more than a bout of jealousy, for she knew he had left her dining table and gone to eat lunch and dinner at Lilian's place. Then, her scolding and teasing had been motivated by such an emotion; now she teased without a tinge of it, because she herself had finally had a taste of matrimony: for the past year she had been the contented wife of a *farang*, a professor of French literature, and established residence on the outskirts of Paris.

I had never seen Lilian wearing so much skillfully applied makeup. In her pink gown, she seemed the happiest person in the Victorian apartment. She was exchanging pleasantries with Pham. Dressed in white, she sat near the coffin in which Ahma lay. At the wake, the stranger in white sat among and yet apart from the matchmakers—some of whom still had their eyes fixed on Lan as their matrimonial candidate, blind to the mystery woman sitting nearby, blind to the master-stroke of their French teacher.

Her feelings hurt by the matchmakers, Madame Françoise set out to outdo them by fixing my father up with Lilian, with-out any of the matchmakers knowing about it. The match-makers' efforts turned into a puff of smoke at the wake, blackening their faces as they stared at each other and then turned in unison to look at the Master Matchmaker.

Good food, Auntie Chao exclaimed. The guests had sat down for the meal, their curiosity about a Laotian-style wed-ding heightened by the food now being served. Auntie Chao's exclamation confirmed the quality of the food and so the few Caucasian guests nearby nodded in agreement. Were they Lil-ian's coworkers or her neighbors? They tried to eat sticky rice with forks. In the living-room-turned-classroom, under the thatched roof, I sat munching a piece of fried pork lung. My fa-ther was nowhere to be found. I put a small clump of sticky rice in my mouth, chewed. I looked for my father among the guests. I saw Pham talking to Lilian's Russian neighbor—about food, surely.

Auntie Chao asked the bride whether she could get her the recipe for the dish. It had been a while since she had eaten *larp*. That's easy. The chef is in the kitchen. I'll ask her for the recipe, said the accommodating bride. She turned to the woman who had earlier opened the door for me. Lilian whispered to the woman, who nodded then excused herself. Why would some-one ask for a recipe instead of more food? Here, let's have a toast. The half-drunk Madame Françoise flourished the empty glass in her hand, her face perspiring. She hiccuped.

I turned to the Irresponsible Tongue. I am tired of you talk-ing grand to us. Why did we listen to you? Why did we be-lieve you? I punched Uncle Chao in the chest. Auntie Chao screamed in shock, with sticky rice in one hand, a fork in the other. I pounded on the Irresponsible Tongue some more.

Auntie Chao screamed some more, dropping the sticky rice and the fork. The bride screamed, clutching her pink gown. The guests screamed. The Caucasian guests looked at me with consternation in their eyes and sticky rice in their mouths. The groom was too stunned to scream.

The matronly chef appeared with the recipe in her hand. Is the food too spicy? she leaned toward Auntie Chao and asked. Did you bite on a chili? I snatched the recipe and slapped it on Auntie Chao's bosom. Take your recipe. The ingredients included, among others, ground beef, shredded pork skin, ground roasted rice powder, mixed with lemon juice and other types of sauces and fresh chili and green onions, served with steamed sticky rice. Auntie Chao, while covering her open mouth with one hand, accepted the recipe with the other. And take back your cheap gift. I shoved it at the Chaos.

The wedding gift was a box of cheap biscuits. It was obvious, from the shape of the box. What good would it do? The horrible prospect of unemployment and forced retirement for my father would still stand fixed. It was a useless gift, perfunctory, crude, an insult. It expressed, clearly, my uncle and aunt's view, their indifference to our plight. What could I expect from them? Of guidance and moral support we had none. To expect nothing from them, on the other hand, undermined our blood tie. Which was already so extenuated. With my mother's death and my father's remarriage, my father and Uncle Chao were no longer in-laws. And that was what it meant, the box of biscuits, cheap, perhaps even past its "do not sell after" date.

Needless to say, the Chaos left the chaos of the wedding. Their car sped off with a thick puff of car exhaust. A piece of paper flew out the car window.

I wanted to punch a few more people. I turned around. The guests drew away from me in unison. The Caucasian guests clutched their napkins over their chests. My father stared at me. His bride stared at me. A pair of roller skates in a corner stared at me.

I went over to the pair of roller skates. I put them on and found they were my size. Lilian's gift to you, the matronly chef told me with a smile.

In a moment I was out the door. I skated on the sidewalk. The sidewalk stretched ahead of me. The cool wind seized me. I spread my arms, going at full speed.

Just then a van turned around the corner. I swerved. A near miss. I could care less. I kept going. When I glanced back, the van was driving backward, after me. A man shouted out the window and waved a piece of paper. I slowed down.

The man yelled out, Excuse me, would you know where this address is? I couldn't tell from his accent whether he was Cambodian or—Lao. I took a look at the piece of paper in his hand. The address was none other than Lilian's.

You're going to a wedding?

We're going to play music there. We're from Fresno, the man said. You speak Lao?

I nodded as I peeked inside the van: a woman in the passenger seat and a few men in the back. I told him I could show him the place.

The man parked the van and the band members began to unload their musical instruments.

How much did they pay you? I asked the man.

We do it for free, the man said. The woman said the band played at weddings and parties, mostly for free because they could not make a living out of it anyway. They practiced on the weekends and often drove to wherever they could perform, to Sacramento, to Richmond, or to Lake Merced. The woman showed me the cassettes they recorded. I was in awe of them. The band members wrote their own songs, Lao songs that originated entirely in California, not from Thailand or Laos. Are they authentic? I asked. Our songs are forward-looking, the woman informed me. The band circulated the songs they wrote, had even spread them to France.

Would you play some later? I asked. I then inquired if they

happened to know a song about a man sending his love across the Mekong.

Oh, that's an old, old song, the man said. Nobody listens to it anymore. He shook his head.

I didn't tell the group it had remained at the top of my chart. They would laugh at me for being such an antique.

We listen to new Lao songs nowadays, the woman said. The songs come from France. Lao music enjoys huge popularity there.

The men carried the drum, the electric guitars, and the synthesizer up the stairs. I followed the band into Lilian's place, even though I would rather not have returned to the wedding.

Upon seeing me, the matronly chef let out a sigh of relief, whereas some other guests might have regarded me as a troublemaker and not welcome me back. There were a few new faces. The matronly chef told me Lilian had invited the Russian neighbor downstairs. I thought I saw her earlier, I said.

My father asked me to have some food, as if eating could make the situation better. Lilian sat chatting with a few people.

The musicians set up the equipment in the living room. I had expected it would be evening before the music would begin, but by two o'clock, the band had launched into their first number.

I didn't recognize any of the songs they played. The man turned out to be the lead singer. But I couldn't relate to his songs. They sounded foreign, bland, lacking authenticity, although without any discernible influence of rock. I doubted if I would enjoy the music, even without the presence of my father and Lilian. In addition, the apartment seemed too constrained a stage, for the music sounded too near and loud. The woman too sang a couple of songs.

The band clearly had expected the newlyweds to be a modern young couple. Their performance was geared for a younger crowd—the tunes light and quick, the professions of love too impassioned for the more mature audience's taste. But then most of the audience couldn't understand Lao anyway.

The guests stood and watched, and no one seemed to want to start dancing. No one pushed the groom to ask the bride for the first dance. When the band finished their performance, the wedding guests clapped, and the band members thanked the audience.

To my surprise, the band proceeded to leave, loading their equipment into the van. The audience, instead of calling for an encore, returned to their food and conversations. And so the musicians left.

It was the chef who started the *lum-vong*. A few women clapped their hands and sang the tune that went with the *lum-vong*. As the women sang and danced, they tried to encourage others to join them in a merry procession. Mostly they were met with perplexed expressions, and the singing and the dancing soon ended.

HUNGER

After the wedding, my father moved in with Lilian. I finished high school and went to college.

In the late 1980s, the Bay Area had seen a large influx of Asian immigrants. By the mid-nineties, Asian businesses in the Bay Area had boomed, with Asians as their target market. I had seen newcomers starting their own businesses, small businesses begun by such people as carpenters. I had seen trucks painted with the companies' names, the grimy, suntanned, ruddy faces of the truck drivers and their buddies, invigorated by work and their pride in it. I had seen others become homeowners, people who lacked carpentry know-how but who nonetheless started with fixer-uppers.

My father found a job working for just such a small business run by newcomers. But I would have liked to see him do better, to run a small business of his own—but how would he handle the details, figuring the tax for instance? He wouldn't have a clue. In my fantasy, I saw the two of us working as a team. Our strengths complementing each other, I would be the office manager, he would handle the projects. I envisioned my-

self as a professional hunter of fixer-uppers, driving a nondescript Ford to scour various neighborhoods, my owl-shrewd
eyes hidden behind a pair of dark glasses, while I left the job
of transforming those dumpy houses that nobody seemed to
want to live in to the skillful—masterful—hands of my father.
He would turn those homes, to borrow a favorite term of real-
estate agents, into "gems." The business expanded; we got our
feet wet doing carpentry, fixer-uppers, then moved on to construction. I saw us bidding for government construction con-
tracts. I envisioned myself as a preppy professional making a
sales presentation in a boardroom, in the financial district of
San Francisco. Small business, minority-run. Surely we would
have a chance.

My father, however, preferred to be alone. Starting a business was not on the agenda. He had given in, learned to make
do. And he was already in his fifties, with kids.

I, on the other hand, ended up dropping out of college after
a year, but was lucky enough to pick up a job as a hairdresser.
It was hard work, standing on my feet all day long, trying to
please as many customers as possible. Ten years later, I was
running a hair studio of my own, Sakura Hair Design in San
Jose.

One of my regular customers was a Chinese-American an-
thropologist named Martha. She monitored a world food program and often traveled to Africa. When she returned from
abroad, she would come in to have her hair done. She said I
should be more ambitious. She urged me to return to college
and earn a degree. She liked to hear me talk about Laos and,
after I did her hair, would stay and ask me questions about my
past.

Why do you dwell so much on your mother's disappear-
ance? Martha glanced at me.

She will be hungry if there's no food for her on her death
anniversary.

There's no such thing, cried Martha. She will not be hungry! She's dead.

I can feel it. There has to be food—

You don't do the offering for her. You do it for yourself.

No, I do it for her sake.

No! It's just a way of expressing the fact that you yourself miss her. And there's no ghost. It's merely a projection, yours.

You don't believe in spirits? Ghosts?

I don't like to think of my own mother as a ghost, Martha said. She's not scary. She's dead but she doesn't appear as a ghost to scare her children.

You would go through the ritual, without believing in it?

It makes me feel better, Martha said.

I'll feel better if I know for sure there's food for the dead and they don't go hungry on their death anniversary, I said.

If the ritual makes you feel better, then do it!

I haven't done any for my mother all these years.

How about your father? Doesn't he—

I shook my head. He doesn't believe in it.

See? He doesn't have the need. But you do. Let's do it this time. Martha asked me for the date of my mother's death. On that day we will perform the ritual, she said.

I told Martha I felt phony about performing the food offering. When I kneel down to pray and bow my head, I know my mother or my grandmother does not come to the altar to take the food—since I don't see them. It feels hypocritical to go through the ritual—but if I don't offer the incense and food, they'll be hungry. I can feel it.

It's not for the dead, you see. It's for yourself: you do it to put your own mind at ease. The hunger is your own projection.

Martha got me talking about my old home town. I remembered it vividly. Because Ahma had forbidden me to go near the Mekong, I didn't let her know about my trip to the pier to watch the sunset with a classmate.

We sat by the steps, drowned in the sunset that dyed the river. Merchants disembarked from a barge, a dark outline against the shimmering surface of the water, like a goldfish's armor of scales. Sparrows, arguing and gossiping, flew in and out of the tamarind tree by the steps of the pier.

My classmate sighed and, hands on his knees, said I should write a poem in order to commit the passing moment to eternity.

About a kilometer from the pier was a temple, where Ahma often took me, I told Martha. At the back of the temple stood a statue of Buddha, about three stories high, facing the river, presiding over it.

The Buddha loomed overhead: the oblong ears with pointed lobes, the broad forehead, the red dot between the eyebrows.

Looking up at the Buddha made me dizzy: the towering features seemed alive, seemed to perceive and know. For this reason, at home I often knelt in front of the pillow and prayed, Protect us, protect our family, provide us with safety and health, and bowed three times on the pillow before going to sleep.

Looking down, I saw a steep flight of stairs arching out to the river, the brown currents rolling by. I felt dizzy and shut my eyes. On religious occasions, monks took the stairs and went down to the river to release caged clams, a gesture of releasing life, multiplying it.

I told Martha that there were many absences in those days, among them was this Buddha, who presided over the Mekong and did nothing, as if he neither knew about nor saw all that fleeing, shooting, and drowning.

My classmate, the one who suggested I write a poem, swam across the river. His family in Laos didn't hear from him. No one in the refugee camp saw him. In fact, no one on either side ever saw him again. He had simply disappeared.

Maybe the Pathet Lao had caught him and sent him up north for brainwashing, or shot him? Martha guessed.

Who knows? More than likely he was drowned. Later on, his family crossed the border. In the camp, I saw his parents and sisters, and an absence.

Martha said she wanted to see Laos. But even if I became a ghost, I would rather wander through the whole world than go back to my old home. Even if I could not find a resting place, I would not go back.

Your father, when he left Laos, turned everything over (the shop, the beds, the cabinets, all of which he'd built, and even family photos) to his employee, Ahma had told me. The employee must have gotten married and lived in our house.

I wondered if they (the employee and his wife and their children) still lived in the house my father had built for us, sitting on the chairs we (the living and the dead) all used to sit on, passing through the door we passed through more than a decade ago. The same parlor. The same air.

While in other parts of the house there were cobwebs and ant trails, in the hair parlor there was none. Every morning my mother swept the floor and, holding a feather duster, dusted the recliner chair, the hair dryer, the framed black-and-white enlarged photos of my sister on the wall (the room full of images of the girl's smile), and the sewing machine with which she made my sister's and my clothes. Later in the day her friends and visitors would show up for a hairdo.

I wondered if the employee's family would realize our absence. His children must have unpacked the boxes stored in the parlor, belongings that my father couldn't take along when he fled the country. The children uncovered my sister's framed blowups and my mother's brush, combs, hair rollers, scissors. Maybe the employee's wife had taken the brush and, after using it, left it around where she pleased.

Of course, to this family, except for the employee, there were no living and no dead, as if we'd never lived in the house.

I wondered if the dead return there, to their home. I wondered if the employee's children had seen the shadows or heard some noises in the parlor, some rustling at night.

I bet my father would never go back either, even if he were free to. He could not bear to see the house. He had given up his claim; he had a wife now. Their children would not know those who were dead and gone.

When she heard me go on like this, Martha would urge me to take a trip to Laos. You have American citizenship, don't you? What do you have to fear? You will be safe.

I would protest against the idea. She would then urge me to do research, to get informed about the current situation in Laos, just so I would know how groundless my fears were. Do you still have any relatives there? My mother's cousin, I said. Write to him, Martha put it succinctly.

For ten years I had known it was time for a visit to Southeast Asia, specifically, to Thailand—not Laos, although Martha kept telling me she would love to see Laos with me.

So, one day, on the spur of the moment, and to take advantage of a low airfare offer I had seen advertised, we booked a flight to Bangkok. But once in Bangkok, I began to feel anxious about going to Laos. Martha had to cajole me into agreeing to contact a travel agent for plane tickets to Laos. I put aside my vow to never return to Laos, and we continued our trip.

THE BUDDHA
FACED THE MEKONG

When the prince was born, he had double rows of teeth, thirty-two in all, and could speak fluently. The king's advisers took these as evil omens that would bring bad luck to the kingdom. They advised the king to exile the baby. They put the baby, tucked in a blanket, in a basket and sent him down the Mekong, knowing that he would either be drowned or starve to death.

Currents carried the baby, sleeping. The basket drifted and drifted. By morning it was caught in a cluster of twining bodhi roots, along the riverbank.

It was a misty morning. A villager, probably a fisherman, heard a baby's cry. He found the baby.

The villagers raised the baby, revered him as a prodigy. He grew up to be a king, established a kingdom by the Mekong, in a land where elephants roamed.

The place became known as the Kingdom of a Million Elephants. There, I was born.

The plane landed around eight p.m. As it taxied down the runway, I peeked out the window, and was surprised at how poor my vision was. What I saw fit the term *mong-mong-lon-lon*, fuzzy, opaque, blurry. I could hardly make out the surroundings: the orange streetlight cast a pale glow around the airport, which appeared to be enveloped in a thick haze, or fog, or cloud of dust. There were no other planes in the airport. The deserted quality of the place augmented my sense of unease.

As soon as I stepped into the terminal, a man came up and spoke to me in Lao, offering to carry my bag. How did he know I could understand Lao? I couldn't help but respond in Lao. I needed a pen to fill out some forms. He offered one. He asked if I knew where I would stay. No. He said he could take me to a hotel. Martha came over and asked what were we talking about. She told me not to talk to strangers. He came up to me, I said. I couldn't act like I didn't know Lao.

Of course he had seen plenty of people like me, expatriates getting off the plane, coming through the door to get to customs. And yet my heart began to pound out of control.

At customs, I huddled close to Martha. The official—a Comrade?—stamped Martha's passport. When I handed over my passport, my hand began to shake. The official looked through my passport. He spoke Lao to me, his voice stone cold. You are Vietnamese?

I said no. My voice trembled.

No? He paused.

I stood in front of him, my heart pounding loudly.

You have relatives here?

No. I sounded weak, shaky, and helpless. He had me now; he knew it.

Then why are you coming back?

Why indeed? I often asked that question myself. To travel, I answered.

He perused my passport. Uh! You are even going to Luang Prabang. He sneered. The man next to him burst out laughing.

My voice might have been shaky, but I couldn't hide the anger in my eyes. My mouth tightened. They scorned me for leaving the country and then for coming back. At the same time they envied me for holding a U.S. passport and showing it to their faces, coming back with dollars and such things as the freedom to come and go, the right of free speech, things denied them as a result of their staying in the country. Perhaps the young generation had been trained to think of expatriates as deserters, traitors, just like the Comrades were trained to see Americans in a certain way; and yet, through watching CNN, the young generation also came to long for things Western, modern, or American. In short, they envied those whom they despised.

You must have relatives here. You are coming to see your relatives.

I said no. I had no one to see.

Where are you staying tonight?

I don't yet know.

You are not telling the truth. You are going to stay with your relatives.

He sounded so convinced—and so sour.

With a mixture of anger and contempt, he stamped my passport and threw it to me and then looked away.

You look so pale, Martha said. What was he asking you about?

I told her as we headed out.

He was harassing you, Martha said. Why didn't you tell him you are an American citizen?

He wouldn't believe it even if I told him, I said.

The airport was empty of other passengers. Martha and I were the only two left. My anxiety became heightened. There were only a few taxis on the parking lot. A few taxi drivers came up to us. Again, they spoke Lao to me, instead of to Martha.

How did they pick me out? I would much rather pass for a foreigner, and yet, so far, the locals treated me as their countryman-turned-foreigner.

*   *   *

The orange hue seemed to have covered the entire capital. It was eerie. Why was it so dusty? I looked out the taxi window. There were a few bicycles, motorcycles, and children running on the dark street. I heard their giggles, screeches, and the loud cacophony of the motorcycles. The streets, in fact, everything, appeared reddish, hazy, dusty, smoky. Some shops had red neon lights glowing in the eerie atmosphere. I saw a computer store. And then what traffic there was became non-existent. The bicycles and motorcycles disappeared. There were buildings, but they were all unlighted.

The taxi drove around a big pothole in the middle of the street and kept going along the bumpy road for a few moments, then stopped in front of a three-story building lighted with a red neon light. The red glow was too eye-catching in the dark deserted street. I didn't want to be seen getting out of a taxi in front of a hotel carrying a travel bag. The Comrades would break into my hotel room.

Except for the person at the check-in counter, the hotel was empty. I let Martha speak to the desk clerk. But then when I presented my passport to him, it became clear I was an expatriate, a local-turned-tourist.

After we checked into the hotel, Martha wanted to go out and look for something to eat. At this hour? I protested. I wanted to stay in the hotel, thinking that there might be a curfew, that or there were Comrades patrolling the street who would stop us. They would take me away.

You came all the way here just to stay in the hotel? Martha frowned at me.

We walked down the street. I pray we don't run into any Comrades, I whispered to Martha. You are being irrational, she said in her usual maternal tone. What would they do to you? This is 1999. She charged ahead.

Still, I muttered.

Didn't you see what they had in the hotel?

I didn't see any other hotel guests, besides us, I whispered. I wished Martha would keep her voice down.

The TV in the room. They have cable, Martha said. Open your eyes. They want to be like Americans. So rest easy. They won't touch you.

There was a stretch of darkness ahead of us. I headed for it. I knew it was the Mekong, but didn't realize we were so close to it.

The Mekong? Martha's pace picked up.

We came upon a group of Westerners—speaking American English. With Americans in sight, I felt comforted. I wanted them to know that I too came from U.S.A.

We could ask them where to get something to eat, I said.

Let's see the Mekong first, Martha said.

We walked along the riverbank. Far ahead, somewhere, or a few feet away, flowed the Mekong.

Once more, people came to the river—to the patios set up along the shore—to taste raw papaya salad and beef jerky on a skewer. Even at this late hour.

As we passed the stalls along the shore, I looked at the people inside. There were a few Westerners. Once again I felt a little more at ease. But when we passed a group of local men, I got nervous again. They looked at me. Would they harass me? Or throw me into the dark river. I desperately wanted to pass for a foreigner, but I knew they would see through my pose.

A tall young white guy walked out of a stall holding a young Lao woman's hand. She giggled. They got on a motorcycle parked under a tree. She held his waist as the motorcycle sped off.

Except for a few restaurants catering to tourists, all the doors on the streets were closed. A restaurant in particular was filled with Western customers. I would be safe there. Martha and I walked in.

The menu was all in French, without one word of Lao. And even though I had not taken a class from Madame Françoise, I could read some French. Martha ordered some soup and I ordered a crêpe with chocolate. I spoke in English.

I felt odd, resorting to English while I was the only customer who actually came from Laos, among the roomful of Westerners. The waiters would know I was from Laos: what would a Japanese or a Singaporean tourist be doing in this backwater of the world?

Just as I relaxed back in the chair, someone nudged my elbow. I turned around and stopped still. By my side stood a boy and a hunchbacked old woman, his grandmother perhaps. The grandmother held out her hand as the boy gazed into my eyes. I was about his height when I left the country. The eyes stared back at me. Immediately my sight blurred. I hastened to wipe my eyes. It's okay, Martha said.

Not to give some money to them would be cruel, but to give money just to be rid of them would be demeaning. The boy was looking into my eyes. The two didn't go to any other customers, or to Martha. They had picked only me. They came to me. It was as if they knew I was their countryman. Once again I had to wipe my eyes.

The waiter didn't come over to ask the beggars to go away. Later on I recognized this, this not turning a beggar away, even in this Western restaurant, was a Lao thing to do. What I should have done was to give some money. But all I could do was cry.

At six the next morning, Martha and I took a walk along the shore. The air still appeared to be a combination of dust, mist, and smoke. The water level was low, baring a large stretch of beach, or what could be the bottom of the river. I looked toward Nongkhai, Thailand. Martha and I would not be going there. At least not on this trip.

I tried to trace the spot where I plunged into the river

twenty-some years ago, but of course I wouldn't have recognized it even if I stood right where it was. Where was the spot in which the robbery had taken place?

A man stood by the riverbank gazing ahead, at the Mekong, toward Thailand. Was he a tourist? A Lao living abroad? Or a local? I studied his outfit. But no. The locals I saw could fit in the streets of San Francisco perfectly. At his side lay a backpack, a guitar next to it. My observing eyes caught his eyes, and so I looked away.

What song would he sing, standing at the riverbank, watching the Mekong, with a guitar by his side?

I could tell him that many years ago I had swum across the river. I could tell him about the Mekong, a river along whose current a villager, probably a fisherman, one misty morning saw my mother drifting by. Yet I said nothing.

It was about seven o'clock. A man on bicycle was delivering milk.

People drink milk for breakfast here, I exclaimed. Vientiane *had* changed. If as a child I had milk for breakfast. Or even a glass of soybean drink. But then Vientiane had always been known for its flamboyance, seduced by all things foreign.

We passed a bakery with its sign written in French. We stepped in—and why was I so surprised to find croissants, loaves of bread, and trays of muffins? And milk! The customers were all Westerners. No sooner had Martha and I sat down than I heard the familiar American English coming from the next table. It was as if I had not left the Bay Area.

In the Vientiane airport, Martha and I waited for our flight to Luang Prabang. Again no plane arrived or departed. The place was quiet. The sky was a bit clearer.

I told Martha I would rather not try to locate my uncle. I wanted to be safe, and perhaps I would have to go through too much trouble just to find him, if he had moved. I wanted to keep a low profile.

She said I would find him.

As we waited, the waiting room began to fill up: several Lao people, two women in Vietnamese outfits, a young couple speaking Japanese and Mandarin, a few Americans, a South Asian, a man reading a Chinese newspaper.

The flight to Luang Prabang took about fifty minutes. Toward the end of it, the pilot got on the intercom and pointed out Luang Prabang below. He described the Mekong and its tributaries. I looked out the window. It was the brown stretch of the river. The trees down below looked tiny. As if he were conducting a tour, the pilot lowered the plane, making it tilt at a slight angle. The Mekong moved closer to view. The trees became larger. The town! The Golden Pagoda Mountain! The Watermelon Stupa! Pedestrians! I could see pedestrians on the street.

I looked out the taxi window as we came into town. The bridge. The river where bloated waterbuffalo flowed by during the monsoon. The familiar streets. A Caucasian woman on a bicycle. The temples. The row of houses. So and so's old home. Satellite dishes on the rooftop! The marketplace.

We checked into a hotel, the bungalow that I had passed by all the time when my parents took me for a ride after dinner. We dropped the bags on the floor of our hotel room, closed the door, and hurried out.

We sauntered on the street. I showed Martha the marketplace, which was busy as usual. Shops, stalls, vendors, bicyclists, pedestrians, noises. I still avoided speaking Lao, avoided seeking out my uncle.

Do you notice the men here have perfect haircuts? I asked Martha. She admitted that she had failed to pay attention to that particular aspect of the Luang Prabang scenery.

Look. I pointed at a young man on a motorcycle. I admired the man's haircut. The style was different from those I was familiar with in the U.S. It had something distinct, something uniquely Luang Prabang, the skills and creativity of the local barbers blended with the influence of CNN, American news, and Hong Kong movies.

I had expected to find the employee living in the house with his wife and children. Instead, the house was a noodle shop. Two low tables with low benches occupied the center of what used to be my family's living room. A woman was making noodles.

I couldn't help getting emotional. I walked in, and spoke to the noodle vendor in the language of my birthplace. I recalled that the place used to be a carpentry shop, I said.

The owner moved not long ago, she told me, also in the language of my birthplace. The owner in question must have been the employee, I thought. How long had she lived in the house? Oh, she just moved in a few months ago, after the owner moved. I asked if she knew Big Brother ——. I said my uncle's name. Oh, Big Brother ——. She repeated his name. She knew him. Where did he live now? She gave me directions to his place. I'm related to him, I said. Oh? A question in her eyes. I used to live in this house, I said. Upon which she burst out, You are the son of Big Brother ——. She said my father's name. You know my father?! Of course I do, she said. My questions came quick and easy now: How old were you at the time? How did you know my father? And so we talked. My anxiety about keeping my identity a secret disappeared for the first time on the trip.

Could I see the rest of the house? I asked her—or rather, demanded—and was ready to walk straight in even if she said no. She said yes.

I continued into the house with a proprietary air. I came upon the chicken coop, and the kitchen, and the bathing stall.

All of which were half the size that I remembered them. The spacious courtyard of my memory turned out to be just a few square feet, tiny and cramped. The setup remained the same. Even the roosters and the flock of hens looked the same. The feeding area looked the same and smelled the same. The guava tree was gone. There were two mango trees by the house. I wasn't sure they were the ones I had planted.

The noodle vendor said after the May Festival (which took place in April every year) the house would be torn down. The place—the pond, the short coconut trees with large fanlike leaves around the pond—would be converted into a resort for the *farang*. The real estate–development consortium she was a part of would build cabins around the pond.

Martha observed the place with a scientific eye, saying that the pond was polluted. I told her I used to go fishing there.

I passed the bedroom. The window, which I used to look out. The self-same window, the self-same bars, which were now rusty. The right wing of the house, my mother's hair parlor, was gone. I came to the door. The door where Mrs. Lee walked through to have my mother fix her hair.

I returned to the living room and found two boys in school uniforms eating noodles by the table. I gazed around the shop. I gazed at the ceiling, the spiderwebs up there. I gazed at the doorway, the door that we passed in and out of. The two schoolboys looked at me, I looked at them. How did they see me? They wouldn't have guessed the shop they sat in now used to be my family's living quarters.

I asked the noodle vendor if she could convert some Thai bahts to Lao kips. She took the twenty-baht bill and disappeared inside the bedroom. My parents' bedroom. I looked up at the altar above the lintel, at the ceiling, at the walls. I felt inclined to believe that the altar was the same one my grandmother had put up, but had to admit that it was not. While most of the house still remained the same, some features had gone. The whole place seemed to have shrunk in size.

Feels like a burden has been lifted off your chest, doesn't it? the woman asked. I nodded yes, slowly.

I mentioned that so far, she was the first person to speak to me in Luang Prabang Lao. Instead, people spoke what sounded like Thai, I said. What had happened?

She said most people had moved away to Vientiane—or to Australia, France, Canada, and the U.S.—while a group of newcomers moved in. Those at the Thai-Lao border, I supposed. Those at the Thai side of the border spoke Lao, and those at the Lao side of the border spoke Thai.

What you heard them speak, she said, was the language called Thai Lao.

Because of this language spoken by the new inhabitants, Luang Prabang gave me an alien feeling, although the physical setting remained the same. Regardless, it was my place of birth, and I proceeded to get reacquainted with it.

Martha and I came to the steps of the pier. A young man walked up to us and spoke Lao to me, hailing me as a Big Brother, offering to take us to a well-known religious site, the cave up the Mekong, for forty U.S. dollars. He would not take Lao or even Thai currency. How did he know I had U.S. dollars?

I recognized the man as the type of newcomer the noodle vendor had told me about. He didn't speak the pure, distinct, authentic Luang Prabang Lao that I did, the language of the true native. And yet to him I was a tourist, a customer. It was likely that he didn't even know the Lao that I spoke was the language spoken by all lowlanders in Luang Prabang, before his days. It interested him not at all, a businessman, how I came to speak Lao to him and English to Martha, how a native became, in his eyes, a tourist.

You can find me here, he said, if you decide to take a boat trip to the cave. I certainly would not pay forty dollars for a trip to the temple that I had known about since I was a child.

And he should have known that to treat a religious site as a tourist attraction, a money machine, was an insult.

Under the tall, far-reaching tamarind tree, in its shade, a group of people sat in a circle sorting the tamarinds. Martha and I sat by the steps. Below the steps, by the river, Western tourists got out of a barge. The sound of the motor chugging.

We took the road along the river, to look for the temple about one or two kilometers down, and found it. We came to the back of the temple. The Buddha, with the long earlobes, the broad forehead, was the self-same Buddha of my memory, who still loomed over the river, still made me dizzy as I looked up. The flight of steps that led to the Mekong was still there. The Buddha faced the Mekong, each reflecting the serenity of the other. The Buddha looked on. The Mekong flowed on.

The moment had come to seek out my uncle. Martha headed for the old Chinatown to try out a French restaurant while I went to look for my uncle. It took no effort to find him: I recognized the intersection, the block, the dust. I recognized him. He didn't recognize me.

Are you really Ah-Ming? He sounded doubtful as he stood in front of the house. He uttered my name for confirmation. He said, The noodle vendor came to tell me, Do you know your nephew is here? The son of your Big Brother. Oh? So why hasn't he come to see me?

Why, indeed. Suddenly, my intention of not seeking him out made no sense. My avoidance of speaking the language, my vow never to return also made no sense. Physically I was in Laos, but mentally I was still saying to myself: I will not go back. I will not go back.

Over dinner, Uncle said to me, I told your dad, If you want to leave, then the whole family leave together. If die, then die together. Why split the family?

It's typical of him, the way he acts, I said. I was thinking of the way my father had combined our household with that of Madame Françoise, the way he wanted to stay with Lilian even before they were married, the way he sent me off to live with Uncle Chao.

Uncle said, Why leave my little sister in the capital by herself, sending her away to Thailand? All women and children in the boat. Not a man with them.

Even when I was a child, I knew Uncle cared for my mother. He called her "Little Sister."

I asked the question in a casual way, by leaning forward to take a bite of a slice of papaya. Did he make the arrangements?

Uncle nodded. He understood whom the "he" referred to.

Again I asked, Mama didn't leave home on her own, did she? Uncle said no.

So he arranged it, I muttered.

He sent them to Vientiane, left them there, and came back to Luang Prabang by himself. The telegram came from your aunt. She said your mother was missing. Only then did he hurry to Vientiane. Your mother was missing. Only your sister's body was found. And he cremated her in Vientiane. He didn't even tell me where he left her ashes.

So, because he arranged the trip, my father knew where the boatman lived. That was how he retrieved my mother's jewelry. I thought my sister was buried in Luang Prabang, and I wasn't sure how I would locate her grave.

He didn't even tell me when he left, Uncle said. He was too secretive, too insecure. Never, never let on what was on his mind.

I knew that all right. I sighed. I decided not to say any more.

After a pause, Uncle said, The next time you come back, Uncle will probably not be around anymore. He said he could see only with his right eye now. And he got sick frequently.

The next morning, Martha and I looked for a barbershop. We found a tiny stall. I watched the barber: could he have gotten his sense of style from watching TV? Martha walked right in. The barber had a wondering look because, in the Luang Prabang that I knew, men cut men's hair, women cut women's. But then I followed her in and he realized I was the customer. We spoke in Lao.

I sat in the chair. He wrapped a big white cloth around me, tightened it around my neck, used a clip to hold it in place, and proceeded to snip. I watched the barber cut my hair, telling myself that I would bring the style to the Bay Area and apply it to my customers.

Now you have a Luang Prabang haircut, Martha exclaimed after the barber untied the big cloth and I got out the chair.

I went to say good-bye to Uncle. We lined up for the photo: my aunt, my camera-shy cousin. And then Uncle turned to a small mirror that was hung on the wall to check his hair, comb it. He was the only person in the group who did so, who combed his hair, to look his best. But his gesture was unnecessary, because his hair was already well combed, well maintained, well styled.

I wondered if Martha noticed my uncle's gesture as she prepared to take the picture.

The van waited by the sidewalk to take me and Martha to the airport. I slung the travel bag on my shoulder. I would come back, I told Uncle.

He barely nodded. With his eye problem, perhaps he could barely see me. Take good care, he uttered, as I moved toward the van. His daughter smiled.

The van drove past the street which I used to walk along so many times; some of the houses I still recognized, among them Mrs. Lee's. The van passed the Watermelon Stupa, and as it made a right turn, I glanced to the left: the street led slightly uphill, and at the summit, the Golden Pagoda loomed, presiding over the town as it always had.